Delightfully clever and fresh! Dodrill dazzles with endearing characters in this cozy mystery. Heartwarming yet intriguing at the same time, I couldn't put the book down until the last word.

— Mary Vee, The Storyteller

Who knew birding could be such a deadly hobby? Certainly not me.

Jennifer Dodrill has captured what, for me, is the ideal spirit of the cozy mystery—plenty of mystery peppered with page-turning tension, exciting twists and turns, and laugh-out-loud humor.

A thoroughly enjoyable cozy for every mystery fan. Watch out for Hazel; she's quite the character. Looking forward to more in the Empty-nesters Cozy Mystery series.

— Debra L. Butterfield, author of *Claiming Her Inheritance*

Bird's Alive! is a cozy mystery with elements of suspense, humor, intrigue, and a hint of possible romance. Ms. Dodrill is an excellent writer and her main character, Peg, is well-developed and relatable to women readers.

Supporting characters provide plenty of conflict, frustration, and comic relief for the widowed empty-nester who blogs. Sticking with the theme of birding, Ms. Dodrill has Peg decide to start a bird-watching club. When a member of her group dies, the feathers will fly. I highly recommend this author and her first book in this series. The story is quite entertaining and will keep you wondering 'who done it.'

— Bettie Boswell, Author Christian Romances: *On Cue, Free to Love, Hoping for Treasure, Hidden Names* Christian Children's Books: *Lucy and Thunder, Dottie's Dream Horse, I Love Mom: Our Hero*

Birds Alive!

An Empty-nesters Cozy Mystery: Book 1

Jen Dodrill

To the Rock, my Cornerstone, thank You. Without You, I am nothing.

Chapter 1

I could write blog posts and headings, research keywords, and create printables for my Mamma Birds blog readers. In. My. Dreams.

Not today, though. My hands tangled in my curls as the blinking cursor mocked me, and my mind remained a void. Sticky notes with ideas and theme words jotted on them covered the table. I squirmed in my chair.

"Something inspire me. Please." I resisted tearing out my hair and searched online for quotes instead.

A comment by a popular columnist had me thumbing tears from my eyes. Her comparison of being an empty nester to serving as Vice President of the United States described my life. Me, Peg Howard, VP of useless moms. My nest was empty.

"But your heart is full," my cheerleading, energetic mom readers would say.

My heart is full, but it hurts. I'm lonely being alone.

I wrapped up the post. "This Mamma Bird has been a parent for twenty-six years. Even though all the baby birds have moved out, I'm still a mom. First, Chloe got married, then Cynthia joined the Navy, and now Carter is off to college. Poof, gone. What does a Mamma Bird do when the chicks fly? It's time to figure out what's next. Any suggestions are welcome."

My words whooshed into the blogosphere, and I leaned back, stretching my neck side-to-side, hopeful my faithful readers would come up with a great idea. Left to my own desperate devices, I would end up a crazy cat lady.

And we all know how that would turn out.

THE FOLLOWING DAY, I stood on my back deck, clutching a mug of steaming dark roast coffee, and watched the birds. My favorite time was early morning—before the late August humidity made my curly hair unmanageable. Red-wing blackbirds swooped to snack from a square, flat feeder hung on a shepherd's crook. Mourning doves scrounged on the ground for feed spilled from the squirrel-buster feeder. The top on it was loose again. I loved squirrels, but they would eat me out of house and sunflower seeds.

I curled up on a chair and closed my eyes, letting the Florida sun warm my face. My prayers were silent, and tears trickled down my cheeks.

Last night showed me how hard my new life would be. I wandered the house, straightened pictures, and fluffed couch pillows. A peek into Carter's room sent me scurrying out after seeing the mess he had left behind. I didn't want to tackle that.

I sat up, sipped my coffee, and sighed. "Today is a clean slate, full of opportunities."

"Peg, talking to yourself is fine. If you answer, we have a problem." Lauree's voice startled me. She leaned over her deck railing, her travel mug raised in salute.

"Ha-ha, you're funny." I waved her over. "Come sit with me."

My next-door neighbor, best friend, and social media manager for Mamma Birds navigated through her backyard. Toys lay strewn on her lawn, and one swing tangled around the other on their wooden play set. She ignored it all and tiptoed past a deflated kiddie pool before she crossed my bare yard and climbed the steps to my deck. She gathered her long brown curls in one hand, secured them with a hair tie, and dropped into a chair beside me.

"Two questions." She scrunched up her nose. "First, have you seen the comments on your post?"

"Which one? Yesterday's?"

"Oh yeah. It's crazy." She crossed her legs and settled back in her chair. "The Mamma Birds are worried you're leaving. I answered a few comments, but you need to deal with this. And soon."

My shoulders slumped. "I'm not going anywhere. My life was so different thirteen years ago. Now, it's changed, and maybe I need to consider another career." I stared at the trees. Birds twittered in the branches, and squirrels played, running up and down the trunks. "But I'm not leaving Mamma Birds. It's, well, like that part of my life is over. I can't relate to young moms anymore. Does that make sense?" I hated the whine in my voice.

"Sure. It's defined you for years. Since Zack died."

"Yep. Thank goodness for his life insurance, or the kids and I would have starved until the blog caught on." I held up my hands and shrugged. "What do I do now?"

She handed me her cell phone. "Let's start with these comments."

Several committed readers had already left suggestions for a new career, including opening a motorcycle shop and starting a catering business, or expressed worry Mamma Birds would shut down.

"I haven't seen this kind of reaction since you wrote that post on vaccines." Her amber eyes lit with mirth.

"Vaccines are a polarizing issue," I mumbled and handed her the phone. "Let me grab my laptop and answer some of these. Can you put a statement out on social media?"

I headed inside, scooped up my computer, and returned to the deck, sliding the glass door closed. Florida critters would scurry in unless I pulled it tight. I wasn't in the mood to chase frogs, crickets, or any other creatures around the house.

Lauree bent over her phone, thumbs tapping out a response. She read the message out loud. "Anything you want to add?"

"That's fine. Last night gave me a glimpse into what my life will be like. Rough and no fun." I settled in my chair and opened my laptop. "It's hard to believe I'm all alone. This part of my life wasn't supposed to be like this." My words ended in a whisper.

She leaned over and patted my leg. "I can't imagine. John and I may never be alone. I snuck out this morning while he fed the twins and got them ready for school. We'll be in our sixties before they leave home."

Her twins had just started second grade, and I loved them as my own. They adored squirrels and didn't understand why I didn't want to feed all the bushy-tailed, four-legged rodents in northwest Florida. It crossed my mind they might have loosened the top of the bird feeder.

I shook my head, discarding the thought, and forced a cheerful note into my voice. Whining wasn't helping either of us. "What's your other question?"

"Have you checked the weather? Hazel is forming. It's a tropical depression, but it's predicted to become a hurricane soon."

"Hazel? That's my mother-in-law's name." I wiggled my

eyebrows. "She is a bit of a hurricane—blowing in and out and leaving a mess. Plus, that dog and parakeet of hers." I shivered.

Lauree giggled.

Hurricanes didn't worry me much since my house sat north of Interstate 10. Tornados or high winds were the bigger concern. I needed to find my emergency kit, stuffed somewhere in the pantry, and refill it.

I opened my blog's admin page and scrolled through, replying to followers asking questions. "Hey, check out this idea." I slid my laptop to her and stood. "Want more coffee?"

She jiggled her mug, gave it to me, and bent over the laptop. I watched her through the glass door while refilling our mugs, sure to screw her travel cup top on tight. At one point, she sat up straight and tipped her head. I picked up both cups, opened the sliding door, and set her coffee on the table. "What do you think?"

"It's brilliant." She squealed. "Perfect timing."

THE UNIVERSITY OF WEST FLORIDA was a ten-minute drive from my house. I had an alumni pass for the pool and knew there was a clubhouse bulletin board for flyers. Lauree and I created one with little tear-offs at the bottom that included my phone number. I tacked the flyer up and waited for the calls to roll in.

Seven people called, but only two men and three women showed up for the kick-off meeting of The Empty Nesters Birding Group. Scheduling it for the night after Labor Day might have been a mistake, but I didn't want to delay my new adventure. Hazel gathered strength off the east coast of south Texas and reached hurricane status that day, which might have played a part in the low attendance, although most Floridians were lackadaisical about anything below a Cat Three.

"Welcome! Come on in!" I greeted each person and pointed them to the kitchen island for coffee, small bottles of water, and chocolate chip cookies. "Help yourself and take a seat."

"I'm glad you started this," said a slender blonde who introduced herself as Carmen. She fiddled with her gaudy diamond wedding band. "I don't know much about birds, but this sounded fun." She wobbled to the island on her high heels, scrunched her nose at the cookies, and grabbed a mug of black coffee. She turned to me. "I think your blog is terrific. It's great how you stay-at-home moms create things."

"Um, thank you." I avoided eye contact with Lauree. Carmen's "mom" comment would have her blood boiling.

When my clock cuckooed seven times, I clapped my hands and joined my fellow birders-to-be in the living room. "Thanks for coming. Let's start the meeting."

A knock sounded, and Lauree opened the front door to our last birder. I waved at her and continued. "You don't have to be an empty nester in this group. I wanted to meet people my age and stage of life. And you don't have to be a birder already. Let's introduce ourselves. Then we'll decide how we want to do things."

Excitement bubbled up inside of me.

Carmen glanced at the others and raised her hand. "I'll go first." She stood, smoothed her skirt, and passed out business cards as she told us about her career as a real estate agent. Lauree cocked an eyebrow and cleared her throat.

"Thanks, Carmen." I butted in on her long-winded spiel. "Who's next? Sylvia, tell us a little about yourself."

Sylvia, a reserved-looking woman closing in on her mid-sixties, was tall and thin with a bird beak of a nose and graying hair tied up in a bun. "I brought lists tonight." She passed copies around the room. "This shows birds common to the area. I've been birding for years. My daughter, Charlene, used to go with me back when this part of Pensacola was undeveloped. The protected wetlands behind your house, Peg, made this a popular place for birds before they built this subdivision."

"Wow." I glanced at her handout. "Thank you, Sylvia. This is super helpful. And each bird's name has a box next to it. It's like a scavenger hunt, isn't it?"

Her brown eyes sparkled. "Yes!"

"I have several feeders out back and recognize a few of my visitors." I flapped the piece of paper. "This will help me identify more."

"You probably get raccoons and lots of squirrels, don't you?" She took her seat.

I gave a toothy smile. "I know what those are, though."

The older man in our group chuckled and stood. "I'll go. My name is Owen. I'm a retired history professor at UWF." His bald head glistened in the overhead lights. "I'm an empty nester and a widower. My wife died three years ago, and learning something new sounded fun. The only birds I'm familiar with are seagulls and cardinals." He winked at me.

"I'm a widow. Thirteen years." *What am I doing?* My cheeks burned. Sharing information like this wasn't me. Even though I strived for "real" life on my blog, I was more reticent in person.

He gave an understanding nod and took his seat.

The other man stood, raking his fingers through his buzz-cut, salt-and-pepper hair. "I'm Shortie."

Lauree snorted. He wasn't short, standing well over six feet tall, with broad shoulders that carried an air of power and authority.

He chuckled. "Got the nickname at boot camp, and it stuck. Thirty years later, I still introduce myself that way. My real name's Winston, but I go by Shortie."

He shoved his hands in his pockets. "I retired from the

Navy military police force a few months ago, and I'm bored." He blew out a breath. "My bird knowledge isn't much better than Owen's. My daughter works at the pool at UWF, and she saw the announcement and forced me to come." He sat. "Next."

We all stared at our last empty nester. She remained curled on her chair and offered a brief wave. "I'm Anna." A slight woman with long brown hair and a nervous air, she'd scurried to her seat when she came in, staying still and quiet. I leaned toward her, waiting for more.

Realizing she wouldn't contribute any other information, I chirped, "My name is Peg, and my youngest son just left for the University of South Alabama in Mobile, making me an official empty nester." I gestured to Owen. "As I said, I'm a widow. Discovering more about birds and finding friends are two of the reasons why I started the group. A blog reader suggested this as a new hobby, and it sounded fun." I pointed to Lauree. "This is my neighbor and close friend, Lauree. She's helping me out for tonight."

She wiggled her fingers in greeting.

A glance around the room sent a tentative hope fluttering inside my belly. No more whining. The Empty Nesters Birding Group would help me out of my slump.

Lauree stayed to help clean up. She'd come to meet the birders and make sure they passed her character check. I waited for her observations. My friend wasn't snarky, but she could read people.

She wiped cookie crumbs off the island into the trash can. I leaned against the kitchen counter, watching her.

"What?"

"Nothing, just waiting on your assessment. Any creepos?"

"Not creepos." She washed her hands and dried them on the kitchen towel before spreading it out to dry.

"But?"

"Well." She held up a hand and counted on each finger. "Carmen is interesting, Sylvia is amazing, Owen seems lonely, Shortie is hot, and what's up with Anna?"

I imitated her countdown. "Not all real estate agents are as unique as Carmen. Sylvia is going to teach us about birding. Owen is kind. I agree about Shortie. And Anna is a mystery."

She hugged me before heading for the front door. "This is why we're friends." She stepped out onto the porch. Leaning back in, she said, "Can't wait for you to get to know Shortie better. No wedding ring, FYI." She pulled the door shut.

I locked it behind her, closed the back door blinds, and set the house alarm. As I drifted to sleep, I chuckled again about her Shortie comment. Then Anna's face came to mind. She didn't seem to fit in with the group. I'd make a point to talk to her on our first birding trip Saturday. I turned over and pushed my pillow into shape. There was plenty of time to learn more about my new birding friends.

Chapter 2

"Hurricane Hazel has stalled out off the Texas coast," the weatherman announced the next morning. "The spaghetti models all show it meandering over the state in the next few days, dumping plenty of rain. Tune back in tonight for an update."

"Sure hope that spaghetti knows what it's talking about," I grumbled. My emergency kit wasn't in the pantry, and I didn't know where else to search. If the models were correct, I didn't need it. Yet. September was the worst month for hurricanes in the Gulf, and I wanted to be prepared.

I switched off the television and grabbed my phone and purse. Sylvia volunteered her house for our first birding trip and strongly advised binoculars and sturdy shoes. My local big-box retail store should have both, and I could get a coffee while I was there.

Inside the store, I grabbed a buggy, got my iced mocha, stuck it in the cupholder, and headed to the shoe area. Sandals were my everyday footwear until October unless we got an early cold snap. I dug for the socks shoved in my purse.

A cute pair of baby blue canvas high tops with solid tread

beckoned me. I attempted to shove my foot into the shoes. Not happening. One more try. From the corner of my eye, I saw a set of men's boots appear next to me. But these had an owner. Glancing up, I found the oldest member of my new birding group.

"Hi, Owen." I attempted a wave and tipped.

He steadied me as I stood, still struggling to cram my foot into the shoe. "I'm not sure those fit."

"Ugh." I yanked it off. "I see these cute shoes and forget about my monster feet."

He snorted. "I don't think you have monster feet." His lips twitched.

"All right, fellow birder-to-be." I swung my arm at the rack of footwear. "What would you suggest?"

Lips pursed, he perused the selection. Even in madras shorts and a dark navy polo, the staple uniform of older men in Florida, he reeked of academia. "Hmm." He pointed. "Those should fit your mon—feet." He caught himself.

The rugged boots with thick and tire-like tread were not my style. "Um, no."

"No?"

"Yep, no. I'm not wearing those. You can wear them."

He gestured to his shoes. "I've already got a pair. Decided to break them in before Saturday. I don't want blisters."

"Yeah, I thought they seemed familiar." I sighed. "Do you think they are best for birding? They're clunky. And heavy." *And ugly.*

"Would you like them better if they came in light blue?

The thought cheered me. "Yes! Where are the other colors?" I walked down the row of boots.

His deep belly laugh startled me. "They only come in black, Peg. And, yes, these will protect your feet, and keep them safe from sticks, bugs, and other critters. Here, try them." He pushed the box at me.

I plopped onto a bench and tugged them on. My feet slipped in with ease, and I trudged up and down the aisle.

"You're right. These feel better. If only they weren't so ugly."

He ran his hand over his head and smirked. "You could paint them? Or cover them with duct tape?"

"Ha, ha, I don't think either idea would work." I added the boots to my buggy, peeled off the socks, and slipped back into my sandals. "Do you have binoculars?"

He walked beside me as I searched for the camping gear section. "Yes, my wife and I took an Alaskan cruise the year before she passed."

I stopped and touched his arm. "I'm sorry."

He flapped his hand. "Don't be. It's been three years, and I'm adjusting."

"It's been thirteen years for me." We continued walking. "It does get less painful. My kids were still young when Zack died."

"Tell me a little about your husband."

When Zack first died, I came up with an automated script to tell people what happened. Brief and succinct. As emotionless as possible. People wanted the details, but they didn't want the emotion. Only a select few could stand it. Lauree was the closest friend who stayed. Grief is the great divide, so to speak.

As the years passed, sharing positive memories and telling how his death impacted the kids and me became easier. I gave Owen a mix of emotions and specifics. His loss was too recent to provide much depth. Three years sounds like a long time to most people. In the world of widows and widowers, it's like the blink of an eye.

"We were high school sweethearts and got married after college graduation. We enjoyed some amazing years before he died in a freak accident. He got caught in a riptide. He was an experienced swimmer, but he couldn't escape it." I stopped and thought back. Those first years afterward were so busy. Packed full of kids, tending to their needs. "My children were little. Carter was five, and I had to keep going. I didn't have a choice, you know?"

He nodded. "So, you launched your blog?"

"You've seen Mamma Birds?"

"I'm surprisingly tech-savvy. I researched you online before committing to the meeting." He imitated tapping on computer keys.

"I'm glad what you found didn't turn you away. We have quite the mixed group, don't we?"

"*Mm-hmm*, eclectic."

Didn't look like I'd get any snark from him. We continued walking.

"I am excited about our first outing, getting to know the others and being out in nature," he said.

I sipped my iced coffee, enjoying the cold, chocolate deliciousness. "That's why I started it."

He stopped again and tipped his head, a curious light in his pale blue eyes. "It seems when something monumental happens in life, you find a way to get past it."

His words startled me. I hadn't thought about it like that. Was it wrong to try to deal with what life threw at me? I knew I always had to be busy and keep going. Too much down time gave me a chance to think. It never seemed like a bad thing. Before.

He touched my arm. "It's admirable. You keep moving forward. You don't let things stop you."

We reached the sporting goods department, and he

pointed out binoculars in my price range. I added them to my buggy and took the opportunity to change the subject, reserving what he'd said to think about later.

Owen followed me toward the self-serve checkout.

I rooted through my purse for my credit card. "Aren't you getting anything?"

"Oh, your lovely company distracted me. I'll leave you be and do my shopping. My hurricane supplies need updating."

"See you Saturday." I scanned my purchases and made another mental note to search the pantry again for my kit.

"Make sure to wear those this week." He pointed to the shoebox. "Otherwise, you'll regret it."

I eyed the boots and shoved them into a plastic bag. "I don't want to wear them at all," I muttered. Owen knew what he was talking about, so I'd take his advice—better than blisters.

THE EMPTY NESTERS Birding Group met at Sylvia's on Saturday mid-morning. Her house was one I ogled when driving down a scenic highway along the bluffs of Pensacola Bay. A two-story, white brick traditional build. Nothing I would have pictured for her. Mild-mannered birder Sylvia in a million-dollar home —over five thousand square feet. It would dwarf my tiny eighteen-hundred-square-foot dwelling.

When she opened the door, I gasped. "This is beautiful."

Gleaming hardwood floors stretched down a spacious hallway. Fresh flowers in a cut-glass vase sat on a polished side table, dispersing a light floral scent.

"Thank you."

I waited, hoping for more. She hadn't mentioned a spouse,

and a peek at her left hand revealed no rings. That didn't mean much, though.

"Have you and your husband lived here long?" There weren't any family pictures hanging nearby.

The doorbell rang before she could answer. The other birders gathered in her living room, Anna ducking in at the last moment. Several footwear styles were present, from the ugly black boots Shortie, Owen, and I wore to the closed-toed pumps Carmen sported.

Carmen gushed about the house and even offered Sylvia her business card. "Just in case," she said, adding a wink. She asked for a tour, but Sylvia ignored her.

I wanted to explore too. I used the downstairs bathroom to see how fancy it was, and it did not disappoint. Everything gleamed and glittered. Designer hand soap, fingertip towels decorated with cardinals, a vanilla- and lavender-scented candle burning, and the end of the toilet paper folded in a triangle.

Sylvia offered coffee and tea, then opened the blinds covering the sliding glass doors.

My mouth dropped open. "Your house is beautiful, but this view ... wow!"

We followed her outside. The deck had two levels to accommodate the house standing on stilts. The first level held a round, glass-topped table surrounded by four chairs with thick cushions in natural beach tones. Four steps led to the lower section, where six soft gray Adirondack chairs with navy-blue cushions sat. Like the ones I drooled over in a trendy retail catalog. A steep staircase led down to the yard.

Sylvia smiled and sipped her tea. "Thank you. I've always enjoyed living here. I thought this would be a fun place for our first birding trip." She walked to the lower deck and gestured toward the chairs facing her tiny backyard, a spot of beach, and the sparkling Pensacola Bay beyond. "Take a seat. We can see the bird feeders from here." She set her cup on the railing and passed out little pencils and a checklist of birds.

"I do need to put out some birdseed, though." She headed for the stairs. "I bought new bags yesterday."

Anna glanced up from the list. "I can do it."

Those were more words than she had spoken up to this point. Sylvia stepped back and explained where to find the bird food in the storage room underneath the deck. She cautioned Anna to watch herself on the stairs.

A few moments later, rustling came from below us. Anna called, "Do you have scissors in here?"

Sylvia leaned over the railing. "Yes, on the shelf by the extra pots. Do you see them?"

"*Mm-hmm.*" It was several minutes before we saw Anna with two buckets. Per Sylvia's directions, one held a mix of bird food while the other was full of black oil sunflower seeds. Anna sneezed twice, sniffled, and tried to wipe her nose on the shoulder of her shirt.

"Took me a while to open the bags." She set a bucket down and wiped her eyes with the back of her hand. "Something's making me sneeze." She coughed, cleared her throat, and sneezed again.

While she filled the feeders, I skimmed through the list of birds and raised my hand.

Sylvia smiled. "Yes, Peg? You have a question?"

"I've seen pelicans before, but how do we identify a magnolia warbler?" I squinted and shaded my eyes. Typical hot, sunny Florida morning, and silly me, I had left my sunglasses at home.

"Oh, I forgot." Sylvia opened the sliding glass door, hurried inside, and returned with several paperback birding books. "I don't have enough for everyone. You'll have to share." She opened a bigger book, thumbing her way through it. "Here it is." She showed us a picture of a small bird with a yellow breast streaked with black and a gray back and head.

"How will we find it?" Carmen gestured toward the narrow span of grass and trees in front of the sandy beach below the deck. "In the water?"

"No, no." Sylvia pointed to the few pine trees in her yard. "See those two bird feeders and the one on the shepherd's hook? Watch them. The feed Anna is putting out attracts cardinals, woodpeckers, doves, and sparrows. Warblers prefer insects and spiders, but they, and other birds, will come to the feeders."

Carmen patted her hair and rubbed her arms. "I hate spiders. Just the thought makes me itch."

"They are important in the bird world." Sylvia's lip curled.

Carmen opened her mouth to respond, and I jumped in. "I'm not a fan of insects, period, but I know birds help keep them in check."

Below us, Anna sneezed again and coughed, and her breathing sounded wheezy.

Shortie leaned over the deck railing. "Hey, Anna, you okay?"

"What's she doing?" I asked.

A bucket fell from her hand, and she grasped the shepherd's hook, her head hanging. She choked and gasped, sneezed again, and wiped her nose on her shirt.

"What's going on?" Sylvia's tone was harsh.

Below us, Anna plopped onto the ground next to the feeder. She clutched her neck, her face red. She fell over, knocking the bucket of seed onto herself. We all stared, speechless, before Shortie shot into action.

"Sylvia, call nine-one-one!" He rushed down the stairway, and Sylvia punched numbers on her cell phone. I followed him, watching my step to avoid tripping. When I hit the ground, I ran to him as he checked Anna's pulse.

Her face had darkened and puffed up. Eyes open, breathing ragged and husky, she whimpered with each inhale.

He held her wrist. "It's an allergic reaction, I think. Her pulse is too fast." He leaned over and patted her cheeks. "Anna, Anna, can you hear me?"

She opened her mouth and made a faint sound.

Leaning closer I could just make out her words. "Sounds like she's saying 'purse.' What does that mean?"

"I'm not sure," Shortie said.

I touched her cheek, and her eyes opened. "What's in your purse?"

"Epi," she rasped.

Shortie and I stared at each other, and then he jumped up, took the stairs two at a time, and ducked into the house. I prayed as Anna struggled to breathe. Not much time had passed since she'd gotten the birdseed, but it felt like hours before he hollered, "Here! Give her this!" He leaned over the deck railing and tossed something to me.

An EpiPen fell in the dirt near my feet, and I scooped it up. One of Lauree's twins had a peanut allergy, and she'd taught me how to use the auto-injector. I popped off the blue safety cap and was about to jab it into Anna's thigh when I saw her face.

Her eyes were open, but no movement showed. Bile rose in my throat. I nudged her body with my foot. Nothing. I broke out in a sweat, dropped to the hard ground, and laid my head on her chest.

No heartbeat. Nothing.

Shortie skidded to a stop beside me. "Peg?"

I sat back on my heels. "I think she's dead," I whispered. "I listened, and her heart isn't beating. Look at her eyes." I pointed. My hand trembled so hard I clasped it against my chest. Spots filled my vision. "She's gone, right?"

Birding wasn't supposed to be a deadly hobby.

He checked her pulse. "I don't know what happened, but she's definitely dead."

Chapter 3

Guilt soared through me. What if I'd had that EpiPen in time? Maybe I was at fault. Owen's words about how I dealt with things flashed through my mind. Did I endanger my new friends because of my empty nest issues?

Did Anna die because of me? Memories of Zack's death came roaring in on the heels of Owen's comment, and I groaned.

Sylvia and Owen joined us while Carmen picked her way down the stairs and tiptoed to us, staying far from the body. Anna's glasses lay on the ground, and I started to pick them up, but Shortie stopped me.

"We can't disturb the scene."

I gagged and clamped my hands over my mouth.

Tears ran down Owen's cheeks. "I wish I had talked to her more."

"I'm going up to the street to wave down the ambulance." Shortie's voice was raspy. He trudged up the yard and around the side of the house.

Sylvia's red face and narrowed eyes made me question my first impression of her as a mild-mannered woman enamored with everything birds. Her clenched jaw and stiff stance told a different story. This reaction was beyond anger. More like rage.

Why?

"I'm sorry this happened," I said, trying to make eye contact with her.

"It's all right." She shook her hands, inhaled, and blew out hard. "I'm fine. I am." But her shoulders remained hunched, and she flexed her fingers.

"How?" Carmen's high-pitched voice pierced my ears, and she fidgeted with her clunky necklace. "She's dead."

"Yes, I realize that!" Sylvia glared at her.

Owen put his arm around Carmen. "Let's go back on the deck." He tipped his head at me. "I'll sit with her until the emergency crew arrives."

"Sure." I wiped my nose on my sleeve and swiped my eyes with the backs of my hands. While we waited, I checked out the bird feeders. One contained sunflower seeds. The feeder we stood by held the mixture Sylvia described earlier.

"Sylvia, nuts are in this mix. Peanuts."

"I'm allergic to them, so I don't buy that kind." She peered at the seed and backed up. "Those are peanuts, though." Her brows furrowed, and she examined the yard. Scattered seeds lay sprinkled in fallen pine needles, with more beside—and on —Anna's lifeless body.

She stepped back until the ground under her was seed-free. "That doesn't make sense." She turned to me, shaking her head. "I don't understand. I didn't purchase that. If I touch it, I'll break out and sneeze for hours." Her voice rose, and she pointed at Anna. "Do you think that's what killed her?"

When the ambulance pulled up, followed by the police, I retrieved Anna's purse from the house to find her identification. Inside it was a medical alert bracelet indicating a peanut allergy and three extra EpiPens. At least we had a likely answer to what killed her, but not how that seed got into Sylvia's shed.

The female officer sat us apart from each other in the living room while the male officer called us outside to talk, one at a time.

Carmen went first, and her sobs reached us inside the house. Owen was interviewed after her.

When my turn came, I walked to the lower deck. Shortie was in the yard chatting with other police officers and the emergency crew who I guessed he knew from his time as military police. The EMTs loaded Anna's body on a stretcher, and I winced when they zipped the body bag shut. Yellow crime scene tape fluttered in the yard. A bird tweeted, and a magnolia warbler, just like Sylvia described, perched on a feeder.

Guess I can check that off my list. Goosebumps broke out on my arms.

The police officer—early fifties with gray flecks showing at his temples and deep dimples framing his downturned mouth —waited in one Adirondack chair with another facing him, the rest of the chairs shoved to the side. He waved me toward the empty seat. "Hello, I'm Detective Sharp. I've taken over the investigation for Officer Morris, and I have several questions for you." He flipped his notepad open and wrote down my name, address, and phone number before asking, "Why did you start this birding group?"

"Well, it wasn't to have people die." I crossed my arms and then remembered what that indicated in body language and uncrossed them. I didn't want to become a suspect.

Sharp leaned back and tapped his pen on his paper. "I didn't accuse you." His stern voice brought tears to my eyes.

"I know. I'm sorry. What an awful day. I wanted the group to be fun, to get out of the house and meet new people. Make friends, not be alone. It surprised me when Anna volunteered to fill the bird feeders. None of us realized she had a peanut allergy." I brushed my cheeks dry.

"I've talked to Carmen Ables and Owen Walters, both of whom told me the same." He consulted his notes. "Anna opened the bag of seed?"

"Yes."

"Who told her to do it?"

"No one." My words came out as a whisper, and I cleared my throat. "She volunteered."

"Any idea why?"

"None. She came to our first meeting, but she didn't talk much. I only knew her first name until I found her purse and driver's license. Her medical bracelet told me about her peanut allergy." I leaned toward him. "Did Sylvia tell you she's also allergic to peanuts?"

"I'll deal with Ms. Newman next."

"She was so angry when it happened. Like she wanted to strangle someone." Her rage still shocked and confused me.

"I'll talk to her soon." Sharp narrowed his dark brown eyes. He flipped to another page. "Back to you and the birding group. Who scheduled today's meeting?"

"Sylvia. She's been a birder for a long time." I pointed to the yard below. "This was our first outing."

"Did she insist you meet here?"

I thought back. "No, she wanted to share her joy of birding, that's all."

"Did she know any of you before that first meeting?"

Sweat rolled down my back, and I swiped at my brow. "If she did, I couldn't tell."

He tapped his pen against his chin. With the angry scowl gone, his dimples were attractive. I blinked at the random thought. *Concentrate, woman.*

"If Sylvia is allergic to peanuts, why did she have that kind of birdseed?" I asked.

His frown returned, lips pursed. "I'll ask the questions. Let me deal with Ms. Newman."

"Also, where is Mr. Newman?" I raised my eyebrows and smirked.

"Ms. Howard ..."

I crossed my arms. "Mrs."

"Mrs. Howard." He tipped his head back and inhaled. "I promise to ask the right things. Let me do my job, please."

"Are you finished with me?" *Please let me go home and pretend this day never happened.* Scenes from the day Zack died kept flashing in my mind. I needed to get away from here.

The corners of his mouth tilted up. "Yes, I am. For now. But don't leave Pensacola without letting me know."

"Okay." I stood and reentered Sylvia's house, my stomach still churning. My purse was tucked in a corner, and I clutched it to my chest and hurried to my car.

I STOPPED for an iced latte on the way home, letting the cool, milky drink soothe me. This day, our first birding expedition, had begun with so much hope. New friends, new experiences. And it ended so fast. In death. How?

Why would quiet, withdrawn Anna volunteer to fill the bird feeders? And what did Sylvia mean when she said she never bought that kind of seed? If she didn't buy it, who put it in the shed? So many questions but no answers.

More memories of Zack's death returned, and the latte soured in my stomach. I don't know where I would've been without Lauree by my side, taking care of my kids. She would pull me off the couch every few days and shove me into the shower.

And, each month, on the anniversary of Zack's death, she sat with me and let me talk and cry. Eventually, I shared more positive memories and fewer tears. It took time, like I told Owen, but I got my feet back under me. Mamma Birds hatched, and I found my way as a widow and single mom.

Did Anna's family have someone like Lauree? Did she have people who cared, who would mourn her? How I wished I'd talked with her more.

I parked in the garage and pushed the remote to close the overhead door. Entering the house, I set my purse on the island, grabbed my phone, and settled into the corner of the couch. Drawing my legs up, I clutched my cup of coffee.

My cell buzzed with a text.

> Did y'all have fun birding?

Ugh, Lauree must have seen me come home. My fingers trembled as I texted her.

> Anna died.

My phone rang, and before I said hello, Lauree exclaimed, "What? She died? What happened?"

I swallowed hard and told her the story.

"Is it a crime scene?"

"Crime scene?" My voice squeaked. "Her body is gone. They put up that yellow tape, so yeah, I guess so." I sighed. "This has been the worst day."

"I'm sorry. How are you doing?"

"So-so. It brought back a lot of memories, but I'm trying to remind myself this is about Anna, not me." I peeled the label from my plastic cup and rolled it up.

"I understand. Do you feel guilty?"

"No, confused, I think?" My friend knew how the guilt consumed me when Zack died. We argued before he left the house. A riptide killed him, but it's hard to tell your heart that when you have regrets. I learned to put any misplaced guilt aside because it didn't help me or my kids and wouldn't change the fact Zack was gone. But it took a long time to get to that place.

"I hate to bring this up, but what will you say on Mamma Birds?"

"Hmm, I forgot I promised an update on our first outing." I hit the phone's speaker button, took a big gulp of my latte, grabbed my laptop, and navigated to my blog's admin site.

"We have comments and questions about the birding group already." I skimmed through them. The blog insights showed high traffic and interaction between my readers—most days that made me happy.

Key tapping sounded through the phone line.

"Want me to give a vague answer for now? Until you process what happened." Lauree's voice was gentle.

"Yes, please." Processing was an overused word, but the best way to describe dealing with the emotions of death. "Post that it's been an eventful day. I'll add more tomorrow."

More tapping. "Done." The twins clamored in the background, asking her questions. Checking the time, I realized she needed to feed them.

"Go fix those kiddos some dinner. They need to eat."

Lauree grunted. "You do too. Take care of yourself. I'll call later."

"I'm fine," I assured her. "Catch you tomorrow." I hit END on my phone and leaned my head back. Memories and feelings swirled. Heaving a sigh, I set my laptop aside and stood. The coffee would keep me awake. I might as well head to the pool to work off some restless energy.

~

Swimming at the university's indoor, heated pool was the one exercise I enjoyed. Florida didn't have long, cold winters, but the convenience kept me from using the weather as an excuse not to swim.

I showed my alumni pass at the check-in desk and headed to the women's locker room. A quick shower to rinse off perked me up.

During the early summer, they offered long-course-style swimming, which equaled fifty meters, the length of the pool. After July, they switched back to its width, which worked fine for me. My favorite lane was open, so I set my towel on the diving block and pulled on my goggles. As my toes left the side of the pool in a somewhat graceful dive, someone called my name.

I spluttered to the surface and gripped the wall, pushing my goggles onto the top of my head. Shortie stood over me.

"Hey, Peg. Sorry to scare you." His eyes crinkled when he smiled. Swim trunks—dark blue with bright yellow hibiscus flowers—hung on his narrow hips, and he'd slung a yellow-and-white-striped beach towel over one shoulder.

"Hi, what are you doing here?"

"Swimming?" He winked. "I needed to work off some energy after today. You too?"

I nodded. He sat on the side of the pool, dangling his feet in the water beside me. His hair glistened and appeared freshly combed. I took off my goggles and raked back my short, red curls, hoping I didn't resemble a demented sea creature. The sea witch from a popular kids' movie came to mind.

I tipped my chin at him. "You've already been in?"

"Yeah." He ran his fingers through his short hair. "I came straight here from Sylvia's. Keep a towel and extra trunks in my car."

"I went home for a bit. But my adrenaline was still going."

"I can't believe what happened to Anna."

"Me either. I kind of feel guilty but more confused."

His gray eyes were sad, and his shoulders slumped. "I wish I'd found her EpiPen quicker."

I placed one hand on his knee. "It's not your fault."

"We did what we could." He patted my hand.

"True. What do you think of Detective Sharp?"

"Marcus? He's not the bumbling detective type. Very organized."

I rubbed the back of my neck. "He frustrated me. And he was so ... hard. He made me feel guilty, and I didn't do anything wrong. We know how Anna died, but not why that seed was in the shed."

"What do you mean?"

A man and young boy practiced swim strokes in the lane beside me, and I lowered my voice. I didn't want to scar the child by talking about someone dying. I repeated what Sylvia had said and added, "Sylvia is allergic to peanuts. She told me she doesn't buy the kind of seed that killed Anna."

"So, how did it get there?" he asked, brows furrowed.

"I'm not sure, but I'm going to find out. Sharp ignored what I told him."

"Peg, be careful. The police are investigating this as a suspicious death."

"I will."

A lifeguard approached us. "Dad?" she said.

Shortie startled and jumped up.

"Honey, hi!" He gave her a side hug. "I didn't know you worked tonight."

"Yep, all week. Hi, Peg. Are you two friends?" She gestured between us.

"You know Kim?" Shortie asked.

I laughed. Of course, he was Kimberly's dad. She resembled him in her tall build and kind gray eyes. I'd known her since my girls were in school. Two years younger than Chloe and a grade ahead of Cynthia, they all attended the same high school. She was one of the few permanent lifeguards at UWF.

"Yes, I do." I turned to her. "Your father is in my new birding group. We've had quite the day."

"Oh? Everything okay?"

He blew out a sigh and toed the pool deck. "A birder died today. At our first meeting."

"What?" She squealed. "How?"

Chapter 4

I let Shortie tell his daughter about our day while I got in some laps. Neither was nearby when I finished, so I headed to the locker room to dress. As I left the building, I saw my flyer still hanging on the announcement board in the lobby. A few tags with my phone number dangled at the bottom of it.

Might as well leave it. Gotta replace Anna. I still couldn't wrap my mind around how something like this happened. Nut allergies, of all things. And both Sylvia and Anna had them. My vision for the Empty Nesters Birding Group included jaunts through the woods, bird calls, and deep friendships. Not someone dying.

Explaining to new group members what happened that day hurt my heart. It was like a bad joke. One I never wanted to hear again. Out front, I stopped and took a deep breath. Pine trees swayed, releasing a sweet scent. One of my favorite smells. My shoulders relaxed a tad.

A wave of heat billowed from my SUV when I opened the door, and the leather seat burned my legs when I sat. I tucked my towel under me, rolled down the windows, and set the air conditioning on high.

Lightning flashed in the distance, followed by a rumble. We hadn't gotten our typical southern afternoon shower, but it might rain overnight and tamp down the humidity. With the hurricane spinning in the Gulf, the weather might change soon—a reminder to keep tabs on its movement and forecast. Those spaghetti models had a mind of their own. If Jim Cantore showed up, we'd all know to take cover.

I clicked the text app on my phone and saw two messages—one from Shortie and one from Carter. I couldn't deal with my boy yet, so I opened Shortie's text, laughing aloud at a picture of a drenched cat lying on the side of a pool, fur sticking out every which way.

Does this remind you of me?

Three dots popped up, followed by his response:

No! Just kidding!

Well, you made me laugh.

That's what I wanted.

He added a smiley face.

Thanks.

I'm glad we ran into each other.

Funny, I never connected you with Kim.

His joking around gave me the warm fuzzies inside.

I buckled and rolled up the windows. Turning out of the parking lot, my gas light lit up, so I swung into a station on Nine Mile Road. Next door was a donut shop, and the HOT NOW sign flashed orange. My stomach growled.

"No donuts. Not right now." I turned my back on the temptation and pumped the gas.

My cell rang as I pulled into my garage. Carter's picture showed on the screen, his blue eyes so like mine, sparkling as he laughed. I took the call, tucking my phone against my shoulder.

"Hi, honey. Sorry I didn't text you back." I grabbed my purse and bag of pool stuff and shimmied out of the car. Dropping my things on the kitchen island, I palmed the phone off my shoulder and hit the speaker button. "I just got home."

"Where were you?"

"At the pool." I sank onto the sofa, propped my feet on the coffee table, and groaned. "It's been a long day."

"What's going on? You sound funny."

Carter, who was so much like me, picked up on my moods and emotions. I didn't want to share what had happened, though.

"It's been a crazy day for sure." People laughed, and music played in the background. "How are you? Are you at a party?"

He chuckled. "Way to deflect, Mom. I'm getting settled in. I'm at the cafeteria."

"On a Saturday night?" What college freshman spent a free evening at the cafeteria?

"Hmmm, how to explain."

"Describe her to me." His voice calmed me. I crossed my ankles and pulled a couch pillow on my lap.

"Tall, dark hair, brown eyes."

"Is she in your classes?"

"She's in my English 101."

"What is she like?"

"She's awful. Mean, nasty mouth. You know, perfect for me." He snickered. "She's nice. I think so, anyhow."

"When will you come home to visit?" Talking to him made me lonely. A hug from my boy would help.

"I've only been gone a month."

A month. A female voice sounded in the background, and I took in a deep breath. "Do you need to go, honey?" *I can let him go.*

"Yeah."

Whispered words followed a feminine giggle.

"Carter? Hello?"

"Yep. Yes, I'll talk to you soon. Love you too." He hung up.

I chuckled, set the couch pillow to the side and stood, running my fingers through my almost dry hair to force it in the right direction. Dinner was calling.

A salad with leftover chicken on top made the perfect meal. My phone chimed a text, and someone knocked on my front door before my first bite. A peek through the peephole revealed Sylvia standing on the porch.

When I saw my new birding friend, my smile faded. Her drawn expression and red-rimmed eyes worried me. "Hey, what's going on?"

She pushed past me, spun around, and stomped her foot. "They think I murdered Anna."

"Wait, what?"

Through gritted teeth, she ground out, "They think I did it." She marched into the living room and dropped onto the couch.

"Why do you think that? It was an accident."

She moaned and clasped her face in her hands. "I know they do. I never buy seed with peanuts."

I sat beside her. Her hair was windblown, and her shirt was sweaty and stuck to her back. Disheveled Sylvia didn't jive with my impression of her.

"Look on the bright side. If they thought you killed her, they would have arrested you." I regretted the words as soon as they left my mouth. Anna dying didn't have a positive side.

Sylvia lifted her head and cocked an eyebrow. "Bright

side?" She huffed, mouth twisted. She leaned forward and stared at my phone.

I followed her gaze and saw the text message light up again. Under Shortie's name were the words:

The police want to speak to you again …

"Why is Shortie texting you?" Her eyes narrowed.

"I saw him at the pool."

"Have you been talking about me, Peg?" She leaned closer, her lips pulled back in a snarl. "Were you all discussing me?"

"No." This woman creeped me out. Her behavior confused and scared me. She was not the calm, gentle birder I'd first met.

"Why do the police want to talk to you?" she growled.

I pointed to the phone. "I don't know, Sylvia. The text came through right before you knocked. I haven't opened it."

She glared at me, rushed out, and slammed the front door.

"Well, I never." Leaning over, I picked up my phone and opened the text.

The police want to speak to you again.
Detective Sharp asked me for your
number. Thought I'd give you a heads-
up.

Yikes. First, a visit from a crazed birder, and now the detective wanted to call. I sent a thumbs-up emoji, then covered my salad and stuck it in the fridge, locked the front door, set the house alarm, and headed to my glass-walled shower—the oasis needed to end this awful day.

Showering refreshed and calmed me—it was also where I did my best thinking. After I dried off and dressed, I got my wallet and cell and left for the third time that day. If Sylvia could come to my house unannounced, I could show up at hers. Questions swirled in my head, and I wanted answers.

Lightning still flashed, but so far, it hadn't rained. The sun hung low. Summer nights in Florida came late. My phone chimed another text, and I checked it at the first stoplight.

Ms. Howard, please call me ASAP.

Detective Sharp had struck again with his commands. He'd left his name and number, but I wouldn't contact him anytime soon. Retracing my morning route to Scenic Highway, I pulled past Sylvia's driveway and parked. She didn't need to know I was here.

I put my cell on vibrate, crammed my wallet in the glove box, shut the car door, and surveyed the area. Sylvia's home was waterfront property, and there wasn't a house across the street. I crept up the side of her driveway, following it to the backyard. Crime scene tape wrapped around the pine trees fluttered in the night air. This was nothing like watching police shows on TV. The knowledge hit like a punch to the stomach.

Someone died here—Anna—and it shouldn't have happened. It was up to me to figure out how and why that birdseed got into the shed. We would never know why she handled it if she had a peanut allergy, but she died on my watch. Regret filled me, making my chest ache.

It was dark under the deck, but my phone's flashlight app revealed footprints in the sand and birdseed scattered on the ground. Kneeling to see better, I found peanuts, some crushed, mixed in the seed. And the mixture was dusty, unlike any I'd seen before. Scratches showed by the shed's lock—like someone tried to break in. No way to know how old they were.

The building was small, about five feet by four feet deep. I jiggled the door latch, and it swung open. Inside, shelves lined both sides, filled with various planters and bird feeders—no birdseed bags anywhere in sight. Most likely, the police took any that were left. A plastic milk jug, the top taped closed and the bottom cut off on a diagonal, to form a scoop, lay discarded on the ground. Fingerprint dust covered everything. The dust from the ground outside the shed was inside too.

Somebody knew about Sylvia's peanut allergy. She'd said she'd bought new seed, so someone switched out the bags. I backed out. I'd have to gather my courage and knock on Sylvia's door. She must know something. Her earlier behavior made me hesitate, but it had to be done.

Thinking of what to say to her, I turned and smacked into a solid chest. My startled yelp met with a gruff, "Watch where you're going."

Detective Sharp's steely glare reflected in my phone's flashlight.

"What are you doing here? I asked you to call me." He covered his eyes with his hand. "Shut that thing off."

I lowered my phone. "I'm looking around." I wasn't about to use the word investigate. I took a step but couldn't see my path in the dark. Sharp caught my arm as my foot found a hole in the ground, and I stumbled.

"Be careful." He tugged me from under the deck and walked me to the driveway's edge.

"Are you arresting me?"

He let go and said in an irritated voice, "You are the most annoying woman."

"Am I?" I tipped my head.

"Annoying? Yes." He continued up the driveway, and I followed on his heels.

"Did you see the dust mixed in the seed on the ground back there?"

Sharp stopped, and I ran into him again. He turned and grabbed both of my arms, keeping me trapped against him.

Surprise shot through me, tingling from head to toe. His deep brown eyes darkened. He chewed on his lower lip, my gaze following the movement. "You are infuriating. You know that?" His voice was low, dimples deep, and his expression soft.

The front porch light clicked on, and we both turned when the door opened.

"Who's there? Peg? Peg, is that you? Why are the police here?" Sylvia's strident voice jolted us apart. She tromped down the walkway clutching the front of her robe.

The detective let go of my arms, and I stepped back, rubbing them. His grip had been firm but not painful. I didn't know what had happened between us. If anything at all. This wasn't the time or place for a romantic interlude.

Why did *those* words cross my mind? Romance wasn't anywhere on my radar, and especially not with a cop, dimples or not. Besides, just yesterday I was frustrated by his arrogant attitude.

Sylvia stopped in front of us and shook her finger. "Peg? What are you doing here?"

I wiggled my fingers in a weak greeting. "Um, I was just …"

She put her hands on her hips. "Detective? What is going on?"

"We were just …" Sharp held up his hand, palm outward. "I wanted to examine the area one more time, and Ms. Howard joined me."

"Mrs.," I corrected.

"Everything is fine, Ms. Newman. We're leaving now." He put his hand on the small of my back and propelled me toward my car.

Sylvia sputtered behind us.

We reached my car, and I stepped away from him, still feeling the warmth of his hand. "Am I free to go, Detective?"

"Marcus."

"What?"

"My name." He took my keys and opened my car door. "Bye, Peg, you head home. I'll call tomorrow."

I slid into the driver's seat and buckled up. Marcus closed the door and waited until I started the car before stepping back.

Tomorrow I'd be getting a call. But would it be from Marcus or Detective Sharp? Did I care one way or the other? My face warmed, and my pulse raced. Maybe dimples were my thing.

Did I even have a thing?

Chapter 5

On Sunday, I prepped for the possible hurricane. The spaghetti models the meteorologist discussed on the news station had changed like I expected, but now, the noodle lines all pointed to Mobile, just west of Pensacola. My emergency kit, which I found tucked in the corner of a kitchen cabinet, was empty—no water, no canned food, not even any canned, processed meat. Carter must've eaten that. He liked to fry it up and stuff it between slices of bread.

My stomach flip-flopped at the thought of the greasy meat. My mom used to stuff cloves into it and bake it. They didn't help the taste at all. When she died, that was the first recipe I threw in the trash.

After I toted my back deck chairs and table into the garage, I unhooked the squirrel-buster bird feeder and lifted the flat one off the shepherd's crook. "Sorry, squirrels." The birds had already consumed most of the feed. They'd hunker down somewhere to wait out the storm. "I'll hang these feeders back up after Hazel leaves."

"Talking to yourself again?" Lauree called as she gathered her kids' outside toys. "This is becoming a habit."

Glancing at our two backyards, I noticed the stark difference between my grass and toy-free lawn and her overgrown, congested one. A perk of becoming an empty nester was it satisfied my "neat freak" quirk.

"Ha-ha. You need some help? Let me stick these feeders in the garage first."

On my way back to Lauree's, I wrapped the hose on its hanger and surveyed my backyard—nothing else to move or take down. I pointed my finger at the two pine trees and huge magnolia. "Y'all have to stay where you are."

Lauree walked by carrying an assortment of toys. I grabbed a handful and followed her. She dumped sandbox scoopers and sifters in the corner of her garage. "Think this one will be bad?"

"With the name, I would imagine so," I quipped.

Her garage, like her backyard, was the opposite of mine. I could park my car in the middle with plenty of room to spare while she and John had to leave their vehicles on the driveway. I traipsed after her and dropped more toys, dusting the sand off my hands.

She chuckled. "Heard from your mother-in-law?"

"She's mad they named it after her."

"She believes that?"

"You've met Hazel. Of course, she does. She thinks we should vote on each hurricane season's names." I followed her back to the yard.

"Oh, my. She'd name one Charlie Brown after that dog of hers."

"And Roscoe after her talkative parakeet." I gestured to my house. "I'm heading to the grocery store to replenish my hurricane stash. Need anything?"

"No, John took the twins shopping yesterday. If you're

hungry, we have plenty of snack cakes." We dropped the last load of toys in the garage.

"Carter ate our canned meat sometime before he left for college." I grimaced. "Not sure why I even buy that stuff. Snack cakes don't sound yummy, either."

I hugged my friend and headed inside for my keys and wallet. My lawn guy had mowed and edged, and my house gleamed. Light-colored bricks and fresh white trim—my favorite combination—plus navy blue on the front door for contrast.

The forecast for the hurricane predicted a hit late Tuesday night, early Wednesday morning, and the skies were clear for now. Rain bands would hit soon. I hoped the store had ample supplies and water.

People on the Gulf Coast tended to be laid back about hurricanes. It had been years since a major hurricane hit. Hazel was supposed to be a Cat One or a Two. With wind speeds under one hundred, it would seem like a tropical storm compared to Katrina, a Category 5.

Parking at the grocery store was tricky. I snagged a spot, steering my SUV into a space at the far end of the lot, and headed for the store, swiping sweat off my face. The air-conditioning inside was a relief. Little decent shelf-stable food was left, but I grabbed what I needed, avoiding the canned meat. Carter texted me he would stay at the college, the new girlfriend playing a part in his decision.

On the drive home, I called Chloe. I hadn't talked to my middle kiddo in two weeks. Anna's death and Sylvia's erratic behavior had sapped all my time and mental capacity.

"Hi, sweetie, just checking on you and Tom. Got your supplies ready?"

"Of course. Tom stocked up when hurricane season started. You know how he is."

My OCD son-in-law complimented Chloe's artistic, go-with-the-flow ways. "True. The grocery store's shelves were getting empty. I picked up enough, though."

"It'll hit between Mobile and Pensacola. We'll get the right side, so keep an eye on the weather."

"Yes, Mother," I teased.

"Well, you know the right side is the worst one."

Yes, I did, and I hoped my roof wouldn't be damaged. Wetlands protected the land behind me. The creek might rise, but I shouldn't have any flooding with the way my house sat up a slight slope.

We chatted until I got home. After putting away my groceries, I pulled out a box of tall, unscented candles, put new batteries in my flashlight and camping lantern, and stacked everything on the island. I was set and ready for Hurricane Hazel.

Monday found me sitting at the kitchen table, busy at work on my blog—another thing that had fallen to the wayside after Anna's demise. Lauree kept things scheduled and interacted with most comments, but I liked to go in and add my two cents.

Marcus had said he would call Sunday, and I was relieved he hadn't. So I was attracted to his dimples, so what? Shortie was tall and handsome and looked great in his swim trunks. Two men in my life, and I wasn't sure I wanted either. What I wanted was to solve Anna's death, but I couldn't think of anything else to do before Hazel hit. I'd already investigated Sylvia's shed and the surrounding ground. My knowledge of peanut allergies was limited, so I called Lauree to pick her brain after my blogging duties ended.

"Peanut allergies seem to be more common now," she said. "Stevie carries an EpiPen for his."

"I knew that. What symptoms does he have? Is it always life-threatening?"

"No, thank God. I can't imagine that. He started with redness and a rash around his mouth. Remember?"

I racked my memory. "Sort of."

"As he got a little older, he would cough if he ate something with peanuts. I didn't realize he had an allergy at first."

"Anna was coughing. When did Stevie start carrying an EpiPen?" I stretched my legs and propped my feet on the chair opposite me.

"He got one when he turned four. When his pediatrician found out how he responded to peanuts, he recommended I take him to the allergist. I wish I had checked into it before, but I didn't know. Now he has one here and one at school."

My thoughts returned to Anna. "She had several in her purse and a medical bracelet."

"EpiPens are for allergic reactions. It could be food, but it might be bee stings or anything else that causes anaphylaxis."

"You think that's what she died from?"

"Yes, from how you described it," Lauree said. "Severe peanut allergies can cause anaphylaxis."

"Hmm. Sylvia has peanut allergies, but said she doesn't buy the seed with peanuts. I don't think they're as severe for her. She didn't react that day and she'd been standing on the dusty ground. None of us knew Anna. And if she carried an EpiPen because of a peanut allergy, she wouldn't have put that seed out. I feel like I'm missing something."

"The police have to find out if Sylvia bought the wrong kind. I've done that before. Seen something and reached for it but grabbed the item next to it. Or, someone switched it." Curiosity colored her words.

"I have too—picked up the wrong thing." I hesitated. "Marcus said they hadn't determined what happened yet."

"Marcus?"

"Detective Sharp." I slapped my forehead. My slip-up would cost me.

Lauree clucked her tongue. "And you call him Marcus. Can't wait to hear about this."

I wasn't ready to explain a possible romantic interest to my friend. My cell beeped, and the screen showed my mother-in-law's number. Saved by the bell.

"Hazel is calling. I'll talk to you later."

"Yes, you will. I want more information on this guy." She was laughing when she hung up.

I thumbed the phone to switch to Hazel's call. Charlie Brown barked in the background, but I didn't hear her parakeet, Roscoe, who thought he was an amazing singer and enjoyed singing and talking over the dog.

She huffed before I said hello. "Can you believe they named this hurricane after me? And I'm supposed to get my hair done tomorrow."

"Can't you still go?" I held back an eye roll. The older she got, the more she repeated herself, and she was stuck on the idea they'd named the hurricane after her.

"No. Haven't you seen the news? The hurricane changed direction. They're saying the storm is going to hit here tonight." Her voice fell just short of a screech.

I put her on speaker and opened my weather app. Sure enough, that's what happened. I sent Chloe and Lauree a quick text to let them know.

"Peg? Did you hear me?"

I tuned back into Hazel. Usually, she ranted and complained about whatever was on her mind, and I supplied the requisite *Oh* and *Uh-huh,* and she'd be happy. Apparently, I missed a question.

"What did you say?"

"I said"—she raised her voice—"we will be there in an hour or so. I've got my things packed. When Charlie Brown and Roscoe are ready, we'll head over."

"Ready for what? Where are you going?" Hazel didn't get flustered by a Cat One hurricane. I thumbed back to the weather app and saw the increased wind speed and category change.

"I'm coming to your house. I'm not staying alone for a Cat Three. I'll see you soon."

She hung up, and I sat at the table with my mouth hanging open.

"Yes, I was sad about being alone," I told God. "But that doesn't mean I want a roommate."

Hazel wasn't a bad mother-in-law, but she had definite standards, and I often fell short of them. So I got to work. Rushing into the hall bathroom, I swiped the counter and sink with cleaning wipes and swished the toilet brush around the bowl. After lighting a cucumber- and melon-scented candle, I pushed it to the back corner of the long bathroom counter, away from the edge, to keep Charlie Brown from eating it.

No time to contemplate the animals about to invade my home. I ran the vacuum and changed the sheets in Chloe and Cynthia's old room. The girls had painted the walls a soft celery green. The cream duvet and plush green blanket at the bottom of each twin bed made it warm and inviting. It should suit Hazel. She'd tell me her opinion, no question about that.

It was the best I could do on short notice, and I braced myself to host my somewhat abrasive mother-in-law, her eighty-pound dog, and her tiny yellow talking parakeet.

I tipped my head up at the ceiling. "You're sure about this?"

God answers unspoken prayers—sometimes in ways we'd never consider.

When Hazel got to my house, she rolled down her window. "Let me park in the garage. You know how I hate this steep driveway."

"Um, sure." I bit my lip at her command. "I'll have to back up and pull my car to the side to make room for your Bug."

"Go ahead." She gestured a *hurry up* motion.

Oh boy, there would be some eye-rolling in my future. I found my keys and opened the garage door, backed my SUV out, and pulled it in as far to the right side as possible. Hazel motored her bright yellow—Roscoe yellow, she called it—VW Bug beside my SUV and parked.

She got out and shook her head, her short, gray hair never moving. "I've never understood why you insisted on buying this house. That driveway is too steep."

She had a point, one she made every time she came over. But I hadn't insisted on buying the house. Zack and I decided together. Deep breath. I could do this—be kind and loving and overlook irritating things.

Like the gray Weimaraner that wiggled out of her backseat. CB, as I called him, jumped up on me and gave his usual "standing hug." He was a sweet dog, just rambunctious.

I ran my hands over his sides and scratched his floppy ears. "You're a good fellow."

His tongue hung out of the side of his mouth, eyes smiling.

Hazel cleared her throat. "Can you help me over here?" She stood next to the passenger door, bird cage in hand. "The drive scattered Roscoe's food." She shoved it toward me. "Take him in and fix his bowl. He needs more birdseed."

Please. Aloud, I said, "Sure thing. Come on, Roscoe, CB. Let's go check out where you'll be staying."

"I hope you put me in the master bedroom." She tugged an

extra-large suitcase out of her backseat. It stuck on the edge of the door. She pulled harder, and out it popped, landing with a thud.

The VW was like Mary Poppins's magic bag that seemed bigger on the inside, capable of holding larger objects than its exterior size would suggest.

"No, you're in the girls' room. The bathroom is right next to it." I hurried to think of more advantages to her staying on the other side of the house and added a silent prayer of thanks for my split bedroom floor plan. "You can use the room beside it for your extra things. Dog food, parakeet supplies ..."

She tipped her head in approval. "Oh, well, that sounds nice. Yes, that will be fine."

Okay then. I opened the door to the house and led my new roommates inside.

Chapter 6

I spread newspapers on the buffet in the living room and set Roscoe's cage on top. The chest—teak, expensive, and old—was my favorite piece of furniture, and I wanted to keep it that way. Even with the dog and the bird in the house.

"CB, do not gnaw the edges on this, please. Remember what you did to my old picnic table?" He had the good graces to drop his head.

Reaching for the parakeet's food dish, I sweet-talked him, hoping he would behave. "Now, Roscoe, I'm going to get you fresh seed." I locked eyes with him. "Don't bite me. I'm taking your bowl, and I'll bring it back full."

His beady gaze held no promise.

"He wouldn't hurt you, would you, my darling birdie?" Hazel bent over and cooed at the yellow terror.

He did bite. The scar on the tip of my pinky told the truth.

"Roscoe doesn't like to be handled. You shouldn't have picked him up."

Deep breath. "I'm going to refill his food." My kitchen island now held bird and dog supplies, treats, bird and dog chow, rawhides for CB, mysterious little bottles of drops for ... "Is this for Roscoe?" I peered at the bottle and mouthed the label. Mites?

She cooed again, then turned, blue eyes flashing. "Yes, sometimes he gets mites."

Well. Thank goodness I hadn't placed his cage on my dining room table. I refilled the bowl and gave it to Hazel. Let her risk her pinky.

"I'm going to start dinner while you put your things away. How does a salad sound?"

She glanced up from the bird. "I'm in the mood for meatloaf. How about that?"

"I don't have any meat thawed out."

She pursed her lips and sighed.

"How about salad tonight and meatloaf tomorrow?" I crossed my fingers. A compromise might work.

"If we have electricity then." Hazel harrumphed and headed for her bedroom. "I'm going to unpack. Tell me when dinner is ready."

Sure, I'll do that.

I MADE OUR SALADS, saving some cucumber and carrot shavings for Roscoe and slipping CB bites of chicken and a chunk of cheese. Anna and Zack consumed my thoughts as I worked.

The two deaths had some similarities I couldn't ignore. It didn't make much sense, but solving her death symbolized a way to let go of more guilt over his. It wasn't logical. Feelings never are.

Losing Zack had a huge impact on our family and me. He'd been my best friend, my confidant, the love of my life. Anna was a stranger, but she deserved to have her life mean something. Not written off as a freak occurrence. Both were accidents, and both involved or affected me.

My conscience reminded me of my general nosiness, but I ignored it.

Sylvia insisted she didn't buy the peanut birdseed, but somehow it got into her shed. What Lauree said ran through my mind—sometimes, you see something on the shelf and inadvertently pick up the wrong item.

Maybe Sylvia had a receipt—some proof she hadn't bought the other kind of seed. I made a mental note to ask Shortie if anyone had found a receipt.

Once the salads were ready, I called Hazel. The lights flickered, and rain pounded the roof. CB huddled close to my side. My little brick house was built to hurricane standards, but the windows rattled from the vicious wind and rain and sticks and limbs thumped on the roof. I pulled the blinds over the back sliding door. There hadn't been enough time to put boards up with the previous Cat One storm changing track and intensifying so fast. We'd hunker down and hope for the best.

"The hurricane is here." Hazel sat at the table and eyed her bowl. "This looks yummy. Thank you, Peg."

"You're welcome." I placed my napkin in my lap, bowed my head, and felt a tap on my arm.

She held out her hand. "Will you pray out loud?" Thunder rumbled, and the house trembled. She shivered. "I don't like storms."

I blinked, surprised she was afraid. I took her hand, prayed over our food and for safety from the storm. CB sat beside me, panting. Roscoe, for once, didn't have anything to say.

Hazel sliced the chicken on top of her salad. "Chloe told me you've started a birding group."

"Yes, we had our first outing Saturday. It was rough." I speared a slice of cucumber.

She cut a grape tomato and stuffed half into her mouth. Around her food, she said, "Rough? Like hot? Birding can't be too strenuous."

"No, it shouldn't be. But Anna, one of the birders, died."

She sat back, wiping her mouth. "What? How in the world?"

"They think she had an allergy to the peanuts in the birdseed."

"Why did she handle the seed if she was allergic?"

I pointed my fork at her. "Great question."

HURRICANE HAZEL RAGED and moaned the rest of the evening. Mother-in-law Hazel covered Roscoe's cage, and he settled down. When the storm's eye arrived, we stepped out front. Sticks and branches, pine needles, and various outdoor chairs, toys, and trash littered the street.

"You'd think people would have secured their things," she said.

"I don't think many of us realized the storm had switched direction." Once the eye passed, more rain and wind would bring additional litter. We had no reason to clean up yet.

CB rushed out the open door and pottied. Poor fellow hated getting his feet wet, and I wiped them off when he came back inside.

"I think you like old Charlie Brown." Her tone was smug.

"He's a pretty sweet pup." I patted his head and eyed him. "Don't eat anything inedible." Like my teak buffet. Or my couch.

He smiled and panted.

"I'm going to clean up the kitchen and run the dishwasher so it can finish before any power outage."

She burrowed into the corner of my sofa while I cleared the table. "Do you lose electricity here often?" she asked. "My neighborhood does all the time."

"Not usually. But we don't get many Cat Three hurricanes."

The eye passed, and the wind picked up again by the time I finished in the kitchen and joined Hazel. She'd taken my favorite spot, but I'd make do. I picked up my phone and texted Shortie.

> How are you and Kim? Had a thought—
> wouldn't Sylvia have a receipt to show
> what kind of seed she'd bought?

> We're fine. Tucked in safe and sound. I'll
> tell Marcus your thoughts.

He added a smiley-face emoji.

I gasped and covered my mouth. Marcus did not need to come by, text, or call me with Hazel at my house. She would ask me tons of questions.

She glanced up from the magazine she was flipping through. "What's wrong?"

"I'm fine." My heart thumping, I shot off a text to him.

> No need. I'm sure he knows what to do.

Shortie sent back a thumbs-up emoji.

Hazel and I both did our best to read and chat while the storm blew more limbs and sticks and debris, along with several loud thuds in the backyard. Thumps on the windows and roof made us jump and CB bark until we finally grew tired of it all. I checked the weather app on my phone around midnight, relieved to see the hurricane had gone north and had been downgraded to a tropical storm.

"I'm going to bed," I said, closing my book, certain I'd only read a page or two. Funny how anxiety stalled my attention span.

Hazel gave a shaky laugh. "I'm glad that's over. I sure don't like these storms." She rubbed her arms, rose, and clicked her tongue to CB. "Let's go get some sleep, boy."

Morning light revealed a pine tree down across my back deck. It narrowly missed my sliding glass doors, but the deck would be a total loss. Several smaller trees had fallen farther out in the protected wetland area. I called the insurance company and reported the damage, thankful that was all I had.

My front yard had twigs and trash, and Hazel helped me bag the debris. Lauree and most of our neighbors were cleaning up around their houses, and we all exchanged waves and compared damage. The one positive of a hurricane was how it brought the neighborhood together. When we finished outside, I checked on Chloe and Carter and sent a group text to my birder friends.

Chloe and Carter were safe and sound. Shortie, Owen, and Carmen replied to my text, saying nothing more than a few limbs had fallen in their yards. But Sylvia never answered.

She worried me. What if she was all alone? Hurricanes—especially a Cat 3 or higher—were frightening. She'd mentioned a daughter, Charlene, but I hadn't seen family photos or anything personal at her house, which was more like a showcase than a home. She was close to the water but high enough to escape the storm surge. Trees might have fallen, or she could have had damage to her house. Anna's mysterious death hovered in the back of my mind. Maybe that was why I had an urgency to check on Sylvia.

Later in the afternoon, Hazel announced she wanted to lie down and asked me to watch CB.

"Do you mind if I take him on a ride?"

She yawned and flapped her hand. "No, he loves riding in the car. Where are you going?"

"Just want to take a drive. See how people fared with the hurricane. I'll make meatloaf when I get back since we still have power."

"Thank goodness for that. I'll see you when you come home." She pointed at Charlie Brown. "You be a good boy, now. No throwing up in Peg's SUV."

He followed me to the garage, climbed into my back seat, and stuck his nose up to the window.

"You don't get carsick, do you, boy?" As we headed out of my subdivision, I peeked at him. His hot breath fogged up the window. "Here, buddy." I rolled it halfway down. "Don't tell your mom, but we're going to check on Sylvia. You can be my bodyguard." Detective Peg with her trusty sidekick, CB. "We can start a business." I reached back and stroked his soft side.

We were almost at our destination when the first gulp came. Then a gag. Followed by an urp.

Turns out Hazel told the truth—he did get car sick.

I parked in a pull-off area a few feet past Sylvia's driveway. CB hopped out, and I found a beach towel in the trunk and threw it over the backseat. Hazel could clean that up when we got home.

On the drive, plenty of storm debris dotted the ground and road. Sylvia's front yard showed no damage, but a big pine was down at the end of her driveway. I walked toward the door, noticing it stood ajar.

I tapped it with my fingertip. "Hello, Sylvia? Are you here?" CB nudged the door with his nose, and I had a clear view from the entryway into the kitchen. "Hello? Anyone home?"

I walked into the living room and found the sliding door partly open. I slid it farther and peered outside. "Are you out here?"

A noise behind me made me jump, and I turned to find Sylvia slumped in the corner of the room, partially hidden by an armchair. She clasped her belly. The handles of a pair of scissors stuck out between her hands, and what appeared to be red paint seeped through her fingers. But it wasn't paint. It was blood.

CB ran to her, sniffing and yipping. I told him to stay and hurried into the kitchen for a towel. I folded it and pressed it to the wound, avoiding the scissors. She grimaced, and her head tilted to the side.

My stomach rolled. "Sylvia, Sylvia!" I patted her cheek. Had she passed out, or had she died? I fished my cell phone out of my back pocket and punched in 911, all while keeping pressure on her stomach.

With the phone on speaker, I answered the call-taker's questions. Sylvia shifted and moaned.

I leaned closer to her. "What happened?"

She lifted one arm, finger pointing to the back door, and gasped, "Stop ..."

I turned and saw a figure at the door. The sun shone behind them, blinding me and masking the person's face. As soon as I stood, they ran.

"Stay with her, CB!" I rushed to the door and pushed it enough to slip through. "Hey! Hey, stop!" I paused at the top of the steep deck steps and checked the area. No one was in the backyard. Before I could return to Sylvia, someone shoved me forward. I tripped and slid down the stairway, trying to catch myself on the railing. Splinters embedded themselves in my palms, and my ankle twisted, followed by a pop and a crack. My head bounced off the pine needle-covered yard, and I ended up on my back, stars whirling in front of my eyes like a stunned, overturned turtle.

Barking. There was barking. Opening my eyes, I spotted CB

at the edge of the driveway, growling and woofing. I groaned and rolled, attempting to push up to sit. My ribs protested, and my ankle lay in an odd position, throbbing. An ambulance siren sounded nearby.

"Come here, fellow." I patted the ground beside me. He trotted over and sat, his body on alert. "Did you see what happened?" I stroked his side and buried my head against him. "Stay with me, boy."

The siren drew closer, and the truck pulled into the driveway. CB whimpered, but he sat by my side.

"I'm back here." My shout came out more like a groan.

After several minutes, noises came from inside the house, and I called out again. Finally, a woman appeared on the deck.

"Did you call nine-one-one? Do you need help?" She hurried down the steps, sliding to a stop next to me.

"Yes. I found Sylvia, Ms. Newman, and called y'all. Then someone shoved me down the stairs." I pointed to my ankle. "I think it's broken."

Chapter 7

I asked an EMT to call Shortie. When he arrived and saw me on the stretcher, he said, "I had no idea why they called me. What happened?" He touched my shoulder. "Are you all right?" Concern filled his eyes.

I held out my hand, and he grasped it. "I wanted to check on Sylvia. She never answered my text. Everyone else did, but she didn't." I sniffled and swiped my eyes with my free hand. "She's dead, Shortie. Dead. And I saw the person who did it." A shiver ran through my body and my lips quivered. "I could have been killed too." I covered my face and sobbed.

"Shhh, I got you." Shortie leaned over and hugged me. His cologne, woodsy and clean, filled my head. He kissed my temple and stood. "Hang on." He trotted off and returned with a handful of tissues. "Here."

I blotted my eyes and blew my nose with a loud honk. CB barked, and I realized he couldn't go in the ambulance with me. "Hey, can you take him home?"

"Of course." He let the dog sniff his hand. "Hi, aren't you a beautiful boy? Is he yours?"

"He's Hazel's dog, Charlie Brown, but I call him CB. Hazel is my mother-in-law, and she's living with me temporarily." I handed him the dog's leash and my keys. "Can you get my car home?"

"Sure, but you do what they tell you. Don't worry about old Charlie Brown here." He rubbed the dog's head, and CB rewarded him with a slurpy kiss. "He doesn't look any worse for wear."

I laid back on the stretcher. "He's fine. Please don't tell Hazel what happened. Tell her I tripped. I'll take an Uber home."

Shortie snorted. "Not lying to your mother-in-law, Peg. I've been down that route. It never helps."

Before they lifted me into the back of the ambulance, I caught his hand. "Well, be careful how you say it."

He saluted. "You got it."

Somewhat reassured, I let go of him. Damage control would be necessary with my mother-in-law.

As the ambulance doors closed, I had a clear view of Marcus arriving. I imagined his expression. He was not going to be happy about any of this.

I'm sure he wondered how I got into these situations, but I had to find out who killed Sylvia. She'd been stabbed, but why? None of the EMTs told me anything other than she had died. Now there were two deaths and no answers for either.

Questions swirled in my mind, only stopping when they gave me strong painkillers at the hospital. The nurse plucked the splinters from my palms, bandaged them, and took me for tests and scans. Then I waited for the doctor.

"You're lucky." He entered my room and held up an X-ray. "You have a stress fracture but can avoid surgery by getting a walking boot for support." He turned to me. "What do you think?"

"You're kinda cute." I attempted a wink, which turned into a slow blink.

He chuckled. "You're kinda loopy."

"Yeah." My eyes slid shut.

"Wait, before you rest, how do you feel? Headache? Nauseous?"

I winced at the light he shined in my eyes. "I'm fine." I shifted and moaned. "When can I go home?"

"Let's keep you overnight in case of a concussion."

"Nah, Hazel's there."

His brow furrowed. "Hazel? The hurricane is over, Mrs. Howard."

"Peg." I fluttered my eyelashes. "You can call me Peg, Marcus."

"Oh boy, we need to cut back on these pain pills." He scribbled on my chart. "Who is Marcus? Want me to call him?"

"Hazel, call her."

"Yeah, I am not sure what you mean."

Lauree burst into my room. She leaned over me, tears on her cheeks. "Peg, are you hurt?" She patted my arms and studied my face. Spotting the doctor, she turned. "Doctor, what happened to her?"

I lifted my arms for a hug. "Lauree! This is my BFF, doc." I tugged her closer and looped an arm around her neck. "He's cute, isn't he?"

The doctor's lips twitched. "She's a bit happy. But she's fine. She has an ankle stress fracture and will need a walking boot. I want to keep her overnight here for observation. She hit her head hard."

She drew up a chair. "I'll sit with her."

"She said to call Hazel?"

"That's her mother-in-law. But Shortie told her when he dropped CB at her house."

The doctor headed to the door. "That solves that. Shortie told Hazel, Peg. And he took CB to the house." He left the room, chuckling and shaking his head.

Lauree stayed with me until I sent her home with instructions for Hazel to stay put. I didn't need company, and she'd already called me twice. True to his word, Shortie had given her the bare bones of what happened when he returned CB.

"She's worried about you." Lauree held my hand while the nurse checked my vitals.

"I'll be fine."

She snorted. "Someone shoved you down the steps."

The nurse's eyes widened. Guess the details of my accident hadn't made the hospital rounds yet.

I waved off Lauree's concerns.

"It's not fine. Anna died, Sylvia was stabbed and died, and you got pushed." She sat back and crossed her arms, lip stuck out in a pout.

Fear flickered on the nurse's face, and she dropped my chart on the bed.

"You're scaring her," I said.

"You're scaring me!" Lauree's voice was piercing, and she frowned. "You need to be more careful."

"If you'll deal with Hazel, I promise to be more careful." I crossed my heart.

She huffed and left. It wasn't often we argued, but she was frightened. The realization I could have been hurt or killed like Sylvia unsettled me. Things could have been worse than an ankle fracture. I might be in a body bag instead of a boot. The thought was sobering.

A tech brought my walking boot and showed me how to use it. I tried it on and took a few steps before I removed it and laid down. I reviewed everything I'd learned so far. Anna died by accident. She had a peanut allergy and wouldn't volunteer to put out seed with peanuts. I had a how and a why for her death.

Someone killed Sylvia with scissors—the how for her death, but not a why. I shook my head, frustrated I hadn't discovered more information.

How did that birdseed get into her shed in the first place? Sylvia's receipt would show what she bought if she purchased the wrong kind. Or someone switched it. If so, who? The receipt was the key. That would be the first step in solving this crime.

Then I could find out who stabbed her and why.

The room was hot and stuffy. I wiggled in my bed, attempting to find a comfortable position. I shoved my covers off and flapped my hospital gown for some fresh air, wishing I had my laptop so I could work on my blog—anything to distract me from what I had seen.

A quick knock, the door popped open, and Marcus marched in. I tucked my gown down, pulling the sheet over my bare legs.

"Hi." I waved.

He glared. "Hello, Peg."

"How are you?"

He pulled up a chair beside my bed and dropped into it. "Fine, just fine."

I forced a pleasant expression. "So, how are things?"

He shifted and his glare deepened. "Quit, please." He sat back, arms crossed. "Why were you at Ms. Newman's again? I don't understand. I'm not here in an official aspect, but when you get out of here, I need you to come to the station and give us a statement."

"Wh ... what?"

He leaned forward, elbows propped on his knees. "It's

interesting to me you were in all the 'right' places at the 'right' times." He made air quotes.

"I'm a suspect?" My words ended in a screech.

"You were there when Anna died. I found you at Sylvia Newman's in the dark, in the shed, with the birdseed."

"I feel like we're playing a murder mystery board game."

"Not funny. I'm not playing anything, Peg." He threw his hands up in the air. "What am I supposed to think?" he barked. "Maybe you weren't pushed down those stairs."

I pushed myself up in the bed. "What?" I repeated.

"Maybe you fell trying to get away. I'm just saying we will investigate all of those options. And check fingerprints." He tipped his chin at me. "Another thing you need to do at the station."

I examined my hands—ink-free for now. I thought he was going to comfort me, but now I was a suspect in Sylvia and Anna's deaths.

"Marcus?"

"You could have been hurt worse or ended up dead like Sylvia." His whispered words and the disappointment in his eyes made me tear up.

I swiped my cheeks. "I wanted to figure out what happened with the birdseed. And check on her after the hurricane. That's all, I promise." I covered my mouth and mumbled through my fingers. "Anna may have used those scissors to open the birdseed bags." A shudder wracked my body.

"You might have been killed. You do realize that, right?"

"Yes, of course." *Unless I killed her like you think.* I picked at my bedcover.

He put his hand over mine. "I don't want anything to happen to you."

I turned my hand over and squeezed his. "But what about a receipt? Have you found one that shows what kind of seed

Sylvia bought? Did you find any clues about who killed her and pushed me?"

It took several seconds for him to respond. When he did, his voice was brittle. "Why is this consuming you?"

"I ... I care."

"Why?"

I grunted and bit my lip. How to explain my feelings? I didn't have a dog in this fight, as they say. But guilt overwhelmed me. "My husband died."

"Yes, I heard that." He stood and paced the room.

I blew out a breath. He needed to know everything. Anything that would get me off of his list of suspects. "We argued before he left for the beach." My fingers continued to twist the covers. "He went swimming. There was a riptide. He couldn't fight it." I forced myself to smooth my blanket. "If he'd not been distracted by me and our argument, he would have lived. He was a strong swimmer."

The pacing stopped. "That's a lot of guilt you're carrying."

Truer words have never been spoken.

I leaned back on my pillow. "Yep. I've talked this out with a counselor and had thirteen years to 'process' it." Now I made air quotes.

"Processing is an overused word."

"Exactly. You understand, don't you?" I tipped my head, brows furrowed. "Why do you, though?" I didn't know anything about Marcus Sharp other than he was a police detective with cute dimples.

He turned the chair around and straddled it. "I was married. We had a little girl. They were both killed in a car wreck two years ago." He avoided my eyes, his jaw clenched.

I gasped and reached out for his hand. "I'm sorry."

"Yep, me too." He let go of my hand and stood again. The

pain on his face hurt my heart. "I can't do this right now. I ... it's too much. I'm sorry."

He rushed out, pulling the door closed with a thud.

I leaned against my pillow and punched the sides with my fists to shape it under my head, groaning aloud. Guilt over Zack's death was pushed aside by Marcus thinking I was a suspect and by making him relive his loss. I shut my eyes. Sleep was the only cure for me.

WEDNESDAY, Lauree picked me up and drove me home. She helped me hop into the house and settle onto the couch. I could walk, but it was awkward, and my whole body hurt from falling.

I lifted my arms for a hug, and she leaned down.

"I love you, knucklehead. But if you do something this stupid again ..."

"I won't, I promise." I kissed her cheek and gave her an extra squeeze. "You're the best."

She stood and cocked an eyebrow. "You still need to tell me about Marcus."

I put my finger over my lips and glanced around. "Shush! Where is Hazel?"

"She and the dog went to a sandwich shop to pick up something to eat."

I sat back and heaved a sigh. "Whew. I am not ready for her to hear anything about him. Plus, he thinks I'm a suspect."

"What?" her strident voice cut through me like a knife. "Well, I want you to tell me all, but her car just turned into the driveway." She opened the front door and helped carry the food inside. CB bounded to me, wiggling his hind end, his stubby tail wagging.

I patted him and waved at Hazel. "Thanks for picking up lunch."

She set the bags on the island and tipped her chin to Lauree. "Dish that out, will you?" She came and sat beside me, pointing to my boot. "Now, what in the world have you done to your ankle?"

Sorry, I mouthed to my friend. To my mother-in-law, I said, "It's a stress fracture. Six weeks in this thing."

She flapped her hand. "Oh, my neighbor had one. You'll be fine in no time."

Lauree brought my food and set it on a folding table within my reach. She turned and glared at me, eyes narrowed and a sneer on her face.

I bit my lip, grabbed my sandwich, and took a bite.

Hazel nudged Lauree. "Where's mine?"

I closed my eyes, waiting for the explosion.

Lauree pointed to her bare wrist. "Guess what? I need to go. Look at the time. I need to pick up the twins from school. Bye." She waved and rushed out my front door.

"I suppose I'll dish my own food." Hazel pushed herself off the couch with a grunt. "I'm tired today."

I took another bite to avoid answering. CB sat in front of me, panting and drooling, and I slipped him a pinch of bread.

Hazel spread her lunch—sandwich and salad—on the coffee table. She popped a cherry tomato in her mouth.

"You didn't buy the two-item lunch option?"

"No. I got you that, but I got a whole sandwich and salad. I about starved last night."

"You didn't make yourself dinner?"

"No, dear. You weren't here to cook that meatloaf."

What did she eat at her house? "We can have that tonight."

"No, we can't. I fried up the ground beef and gave it to Charlie Brown."

I took the final bite of my food, pushed myself to my feet, and picked up my bowl of soup. "I'm going to put this in the refrigerator and go into my room." I needed to lie down. A nap would help. Not just my ankle, but hopefully, my patience level. If nothing else, I'd have a few minutes to myself.

She shoved her cup my way. "Can you refill this first?"

Chapter 8

Before the sun rose the next morning, I hobbled to the back door, with a plan to sit on the deck for a bit. Opening the blinds, I remembered the tree damage. I sighed and headed for the front porch and the old wicker rocker.

Outside, I found CB and Hazel sound asleep and snoring. My home had been invaded, and I didn't like it. I huffed, went back into the house, and shut the door.

I looked up. "I could complain, but how about this? Show me what You want me to learn, God."

Fighting against Him and His will had never worked before and wouldn't now.

New plan for the day. First, read my Bible and enjoy my coffee. Later, I'd sit on the front porch.

Reading and the strong java cleared my mind and sent my day in a new direction. I pulled a notepad and pen out of my Bible cover's pocket. Numbering down the left side, I wrote short questions next to each.

1. Birdseed at Sylvia's?
2. Receipt for which kind?

3. Sylvia's killer?
4. Why was she killed?

After circling "Why," I read over my list and added a number five—Did the person who killed Sylvia and pushed me down the deck stairs have my address?

Because that worried me. Even more than Marcus thinking I killed Sylvia.

I needed to call Marcus and ask him. Find out if he thought my fears were valid. But that would mean a trip to the police station.

Or ...

I wiped my hands, shaking and clammy from worrying, on my shorts, grabbed my phone, and texted Shortie.

> Hi, thanks for helping out with CB the other day.

How are you? I wanted to call yesterday but got tied up. Can I come by?

Hmm, what would my mother-in-law say if he came to the house? It was my house, and Zack had been gone for over thirteen years. But Hazel was his mother and might feel possessive. I wasn't sure what to do.

Hazel was great Tuesday. She told me to stop by anytime.

Well, that settled that.

> Give me thirty minutes.

It took me over half an hour to hop into the bathroom and maneuver my way into shorts and a T-shirt. I dragged a brush through my hair, wishing it were long enough to pull up.

Peering into the mirror, I found new lines beside my eyes and mouth.

"Stress, it's just stress." I smoothed them with my fingers, but they sprang right back.

Once I was ready, I found Shortie sitting on the front steps chatting with Hazel and patting CB.

He shaded his eyes with one hand. "Hey there."

"Want to come in? Kind of hard to sit on the porch steps with this boot."

"Sure." He touched Hazel's shoulder. "Need anything?"

She beamed. "No, thank you."

Shortie and I settled on the couch, and I propped my boot on the coffee table. "You've got her tamed."

"She wants attention, Peg. Someone to talk to."

"If she'd quit ordering me around, that would help."

He patted his legs. "Anywho, what's up? How are you?"

"The pain pills help. This walking boot is my companion for six weeks, and I'm sore from falling. Fun times." I wiggled to a more comfortable position. "I wanted to ask you something."

"What?"

I showed him my notepad. "I wrote these questions. Do you think I should be worried?" I tapped my pen against the last one.

He read through my list. "I doubt the person who pushed you knows who you are or where you live. But I understand your concern. I don't have any power with the local police, but I'll suggest to Detective Sharp they send a car around more often for the next few days."

"Hmm. Well, that might help, but Marcus came by the hospital. I'm on his suspect list. I didn't think about my own safety then."

"You? A suspect?" He barked a laugh. "And you call him

Marcus?" He leaned away from me, a curious expression on his face.

"Ugh." I wrinkled my nose. "Pass. Next question."

"Why does he think you killed Sylvia?"

"Because I was there when she was killed. Maybe I did it, then threw myself down the stairs?" I shrugged and rolled my eyes. "He wants me to go give my statement and be fingerprinted."

He rubbed his chin. "You need to do that soon and clear your name. That makes this more mysterious." He reached into his back pocket and frowned. "I guess it's still in the car. Stay right there."

He returned with a section of the *Pensacola News Journal*, handed it to me, and pointed to an article. "You might want to read this."

The headline read: "PPD Seeks Person in Alleged Break-In and Murder." The short article contained few details except for explaining the Pensacola Police Department was searching for Sylvia's killer. It provided a phone number for Crime Stoppers for anyone with information.

"I wonder how much they'll be able to find out."

"Well, they are the police, so ..." He spread his hands.

"I tried to explain this to Mar ... Detective Sharp. It's this guilt. Do you understand?" I tapped my chest.

"To an extent, yes. But we didn't do anything wrong." He stretched his legs out, crossing them at the ankles. "Even when you found Sylvia, you tried to help her."

"Yes, I did try to help her, not kill her." I ran my hands through my hair. "I'm going to solve this case. Wait and see."

The front door opened as I spoke, and CB bounded inside, followed by Hazel.

"Solve what case?" she said.

A sigh escaped. "I want to find out who pushed me."

"What about that woman who died?"

"The police are investigating Sylvia's death," I said with a scowl.

"Wasn't her name Anna?"

Uh-oh. I cleared my throat. "Yes. Um, Anna and Sylvia died."

She sank into the couch next to me. "What? Wait a minute. Back up and tell me everything."

After I filled her in, she got a spiral notebook and pen from her room. She licked her finger and flipped to an empty page. "First, we should find Sylvia's receipt for the birdseed." She copied my questions and circled that one. "Then we can tell if she bought the wrong kind, in which case there isn't a mystery about Anna's death." She slammed her notebook shut.

"I agree." I shifted on the couch and groaned. *How to tell her I was a suspect in the whole thing? And did I really want a sidekick in my investigation?*

Shortie stood. "Let's let Peg rest. Then we'll come back together and brainstorm."

I leaned my head back. "Thanks, I'm beat."

"Here, turn around and stretch out on the couch." Hazel placed a pillow under my boot. She fluttered her eyelashes at Shortie. "How about we go get some lunch?"

"Can we bring you something back?" Shortie asked.

Hazel flapped her hand. "She'll be fine. Let me stop in the little girls' room, and we'll go. You can ride with me."

She left the room, and I burst out laughing.

"Enjoy riding in the parakeet bug." I fanned my face as the giggles consumed me.

"Huh?"

Hazel reappeared and hooked her arm through his. "Come on now. Have you ever ridden in a VW Bug? I need to stop by my house too. I've not had a chance to check it for damage after the hurricane." She pointed to me with her thumb. "This one ended up in the hospital and took all my time."

Shortie crossed his eyes and stuck his tongue out at me as she dragged him from the room. I lay back and sighed. Hazel had a point. If Sylvia bought the wrong seed, there was only one murder to investigate.

And, maybe Hazel's house would be fine, and she could move back home.

I fidgeted until I found a comfortable position and fell asleep. My dreams, filled with mysterious figures chasing me, peanuts raining from the sky, and handcuffs on my wrists, were interrupted when CB barked, Roscoe sang, and the garage door opened. Swinging my feet off the couch, I pushed up to sit and ran my fingers through my hair.

Hazel entered first. "Don't you look like something the cat dragged in."

I opened my mouth in retort, then thought better of it.

Shortie handed me a foam takeout container "Here, we brought you back something from that little café that serves brunch."

My stomach growled at the yummy smells as I set the food on the coffee table. "Thank you. I'm going to use the bathroom. Will you protect that from the dog?"

He nodded, and I hobbled to my bathroom. I leaned against the counter and peered at my reflection. Dark circles hung beneath my eyes. I splashed my face with cold water, brushed my teeth, and combed my hair. Feeling a little more human, I returned to the living room. My lunch, Hazel, CB, and Shortie, were missing.

I spotted the three of them through the front window, and my food sat on the island. With relief, I took it to the dining table and dug in. I was mid-bite when Hazel and CB came back inside.

"This is yummy. Thank you."

"Shortie insisted on the avocado toast and a power wrap for you. Don't eat too much, or that avocado will make you fat." She wrinkled her nose.

Hazel's mood swings were making me crazy. I swallowed and dipped my wrap into the cup of pico de gallo. The café was, in my estimation, one of the best on Nine Mile Road.

She opened the refrigerator and set a cup on the counter. She leaned over, sniffed, and made a face. "He also ordered this green drink. It looks awful, but it smells all right."

"Do you mind bringing it to me?" It was a kale juice blend, one of my favorites, a combination of kale, Fuji apple, English cucumber, and lemon. My mouth watered.

She plopped it in front of me.

"Thanks. Where did Shortie go?"

"Someone called him, and he had to leave." She pulled a chair out and sat beside me, chin in her hand. Her expression softened. "He's so sweet."

I took advantage of her calmer mood. "How was your house?"

"I'm going to need a new roof. I'll have to stay here until then." She didn't ask or apologize. Just stated it as a fact.

I swallowed a sigh. "You're always welcome here." CB woofed and wagged his tail. What a gentle doggie. He'd wormed his way into my heart. "Hey, let's review those questions and see where to start on our investigation."

She retrieved her notebook and pen from her room. "I thought of some ideas at lunch too."

I ate while she talked. Finding Sylvia's receipt would determine whether Anna died by mistake or not. I didn't think she was the intended victim, and Hazel agreed.

"A killer would not know Anna would go Saturday, let

alone put the seed out." She scraped her chair back and stood. "I'll grab my keys, and we can go to Sylvia's house."

I made a face and pointed to my walking boot. "Not sure I can maneuver that well. I need to find a shoe that is even with this for my other foot. Otherwise, I'm all out of whack, and that hurts worse."

"Tennis shoes? I'll drive and help you." She took my lunch and closed the box. "I'll put this in the refrigerator. You can eat it for dinner."

I grabbed my juice and gulped it before she snatched it too. "You know breaking into her house is illegal, right?"

Hazel fluttered her eyelashes. "Why, officer, I didn't realize this was a crime scene."

She was going to get me in trouble. I could feel it.

YELLOW CRIME SCENE tape stood between us and Sylvia's house. Hazel lifted it and scurried under, holding it high for me to shuffle beneath. She knocked and tried to open the door, but it was locked. She reached into her purse and drew out a credit card.

"I saw this in a movie." She inserted the card between the doorknob and the door frame, bent it toward the handle, and then shifted it back. The card slipped under the latch. She twisted the knob, and the door swung wide.

My mouth dropped open. "You are a woman of many surprises."

"Thank you." She tiptoed into the house, and I followed, my boot tapping every other step.

Nothing had changed since I'd been here last, but I noticed things I hadn't then. The cut-glass vase from the side table lay in pieces on the floor, surrounded by dead flowers. Standing water marred the flooring, and we skirted it.

"Her body was in the living room," I said.

Hazel peeked into the room and continued down the hall to the kitchen. "Where would she keep receipts?"

I stuck my head in the doorway to the living room and shivered. Visions of Sylvia bleeding and dying filled my mind, even though her body had been removed.

"Hey," Hazel called. "Come back here."

I found her in the kitchen holding a purse with a paper towel around her fingers. "Can fingerprints show on a purse strap? I want to be cautious."

Said the woman who unlocked the door with a credit card. "No idea. Do you think her receipts will be in there?"

She set the bag—a designer brand—on the counter and unzipped it. She wrapped another paper towel around her other hand and rifled through the contents.

"Here's her wallet." She peeked through it, set it aside, and reached back into the purse. "Ah, hah!" She pulled out a packet of letters rubber-banded together and held them up. "I don't see any receipts in here, but I found these."

While she was busy, I checked out the immaculate and expensive kitchen filled with top-of-the-line stainless steel appliances and a high-end refrigerator with double drawers on the bottom. Those models retailed for over fifteen thousand dollars. Next to the fridge sat a small, cream-colored antique desk.

Papers covered the desktop. I picked up the ones on top and scanned the dates. Sylvia mentioned she'd bought the new seed before our bird outing. That meant before Saturday the eleventh.

I held up a receipt from the local farm supply store. "Hazel, I think I found the proof we need. This one is from two days before our birding trip and shows she did buy seed without peanuts. Let's go to the store and see if that bag is beside one with nuts. That way, we can confirm if she bought the wrong one."

Hazel patted her purse. "I put that bundle of letters in here."

I hoped between the receipts and the letters, I could clear my name. I hooked my arm through hers, tugging her toward the front door. Before we got there, a shadow crossed the window, and someone banged on the door.

"Open up. This is the police."

I recognized that voice. Marcus had arrived.

Chapter 9

Hazel's eyes bugged out, and she raised her arms. "What do we do?"

I elbowed her. "We're not under arrest." *But we might be.* "Let's go out on the deck." I tugged her arm, and we made our way toward the sliding door.

The front door crashed open, and Marcus barked, "Really, Peg?"

My shoulders dropped. How to spin this? A nudge in my spirit, and I knew I had to tell the truth.

Hopping in a circle, I faced him and waved. "Hi."

"You two are lucky it's me," he growled.

"What made you stop?"

"The bright yellow VW Bug in the driveway."

My sidekick stepped forward and tried the eyelash flutter on him. "That's mine." She put her hand out. "I'm Hazel, and you are?"

Marcus shook it once. "Detective Sharp, ma'am." Hands on hips and expression blank, he didn't appear affected by Hazel's simpering.

"We were trying to find the receipt." My stomach sank as I

remembered his command to go to the police station for fingerprinting and to give my statement.

He stared at me.

I hobbled toward him and waved the paper. "I'm telling the truth. Sylvia bought seed without peanuts. Hazel and I want to go to the local farm supply store to see if those bags sit next to the ones with them. We think Sylvia picked up the wrong bag."

Marcus spoke through gritted teeth. "You might be surprised, but we, the Pensacola Police Department, thought of that too."

My arm dropped. "Have you gone to the store yet? We can do that for you." I offered my sweetest smile.

He put one hand on my shoulder and one on Hazel's and propelled us toward the front door. "Y'all need to leave. Let the police do their job. Oh, and Peg, I'm still waiting for your statement. I haven't forgotten." He tipped his head, brows furrowed. "How did you break in anyhow?"

Oh boy. "Well, the door was locked."

"I did it." Hazel jumped in. "With a credit card."

He pointed. "Leave, please. And Peg." He held out his hand. "I need that receipt."

"That was so much fun!" Hazel clapped and wiggled in her seat.

"Start the car. Let's go home." I couldn't believe Marcus found us investigating—after he told me not to.

She fired up her car and tooted the horn at Marcus. He stood on the front porch watching us, arms crossed, no sign of the dimple. My stomach sank at his stony glare.

She motored down Scenic Highway, straight past the interstate.

"You missed our exit." I pointed behind us.

"The farm supply store is on Nine Mile Road. We can still check out how they place those birdseed bags. That's not a crime." She giggled.

Not like breaking into a house. I flexed my shoulders and tried to relax. "He could have arrested us."

She bounced in her seat. "Isn't this exciting? I haven't had this much fun in years."

"I've created a monster," I mumbled.

It turns out the two different birdseeds were not side-by-side. Someone wanted Sylvia dead and switched her birdseed. When the seed she was allergic to didn't do it, that person returned and murdered her.

I've watched enough crime shows to realize killing a person by stabbing is more personal than using a gun or poison.

"Wonder where the scissors came from." I shuddered every time I remembered them stuck in Sylvia's belly.

"Me too. Did the killer grab them from Sylvia's kitchen? Should we go back?" Hazel pulled into my driveway.

"No, not a good idea. Plus, Anna used scissors to open the birdseed. They might be the same pair. Anyhow, Marcus is onto us now."

Her eyebrows raised. "Marcus? You're on a first-name basis with him? And I noticed he called you Peg."

"I just met him." I unbuckled and hurried into the house.

She followed me inside, still talking.

"What?"

"I said," she raised her voice, "we should find out who kills with knives most often—men or women. I'll get my laptop."

My mother-in-law continued to surprise me. She searched the internet while I made dinner.

"Hmm, this study found women use knives to kill more

than men. It wasn't a knife, but close enough. It also says they usually kill someone they're close to, or they'd been hurt by, and often it happens in the person's home." Excitement radiated from her.

"This is it, Peg." She closed her laptop with a snap. "We need to search for a woman Sylvia knew. A person she hurt. Let's make a list." Hazel grabbed her notebook and pen.

She settled at the dining table while I set out bowls of tomato soup and crackers.

"Thank you." She slipped CB a cracker and patted his head. "Down." She pointed, and he lay on the carpet. She bowed her head and held her hand out. "Pray, please."

While we ate, we discussed possible suspects.

"Didn't you say she had a daughter?"

"Charlene. She mentioned her at the first meeting." I nibbled a cracker. "It's hard to imagine her daughter killed her."

Hazel scribbled 'Charlene' in her notebook. "That's because you're thinking like a normal person. Sylvia wasn't normal. Someone hated her enough to kill her. Stab her."

I shuddered. My tomato soup had lost its appeal. I pushed my bowl away and stood. "I'm going to stretch out on the couch. Can you clean up?"

"I'll stack the dishes in the sink for you."

Thanks.

After she rinsed and stacked our bowls, she said, "I'm going to take CB for a quick walk and then clean Roscoe's cage."

I spent the rest of the evening on the couch with my foot propped up. It had only been two days since my accident. The doctor's orders included lots of rest, and I definitely hadn't done that. Hazel puttered around the kitchen and cleaned

Roscoe's bed before settling onto the chaise lounge with a book.

At nine, I decided to head to bed. I'd pushed myself up and told Hazel good night when my cell phone rang.

"It says 'Private.'"

She rubbed her hands together. "Answer it. Maybe it's the killer."

Not exactly who I wanted to talk to. I hit the answer button. "Hello?"

"You need to stay away from Sylvia's house." The caller's voice, gruff and nasally, was unidentifiable.

"What?" I broke out in a cold sweat.

"You heard me. Keep away." The caller hung up.

"Who was it? You don't look so good."

I set my phone on the coffee table and stared at it. My knees were weak, and I collapsed on the couch. "I don't know who it was. The person said to stay away from Sylvia's. That was weird. I couldn't tell if it was a man or a woman." I shoved my shaking hands under my thighs before I realized my entire body was shaking.

Hazel got her notebook and pen. Turning to the page where she'd written Charlene as a suspect, she added 'mystery caller.' "Who could it be? Do you think it was Charlene?"

My cell rang again before I answered. We stared at each other.

"Does it show a number?" she whispered.

"Yes," I whispered back. I hit accept. "Hello?" My voice came out forceful and stern.

There was a pause before the caller said, "Hi, I'm calling about the birding group. I found your flyer at the UWF pool."

A breath whooshed out of me. I swiped a hand across my forehead and mouthed, *It's a woman about the birding group.*

"Are you interested in coming to a meeting? We just started." I wasn't going to mention dead bodies.

She told me her name, and I said I'd text her with our next meeting time and place and hung up, struggling to keep my voice normal.

Hazel's eyebrows almost touched her hairline. "You're still going to go watch birds?"

"Of course. That wasn't the problem."

"True." A slow smile crossed her face. "When's your next outing?"

"I'll send a text, figure that out, and tell her, Marla." I gestured to my phone.

She nodded several times. "I'm coming too. Someone needs to be on the lookout for the killer."

Shortie, Owen, and Carmen were interested in another birding adventure but, as Shortie put it, 'less on the adventurous side.' I texted Marla, our new birder, and told her to meet us on Saturday in the Fort Barrancas Visitor Center parking lot at Naval Air Station Pensacola.

I spent most of Friday working on my blog, updating things, and responding to comments. It irritated me how much I'd neglected it. After spending countless hours writing and creating the first several years, my time online now was more sporadic. Thank goodness for Lauree, or who knew where my blog would be?

Mid-morning Saturday, Hazel and I headed for the Navy base. She drove her car, but we left CB behind. I gave him a firm talking-to, his sweet doggy eyes assuring me the house would be fine when we got home. I had my doubts.

"Did you ever tell anyone about your mysterious caller?" She turned left.

I picked the skin around my thumbnail and sighed. "No. I'm afraid to."

"Why?"

"It'll make it seem real."

She cocked her head. "It is real, Peg. That person threatened you."

"Well, sort of. They told me to stay away. And I have."

She huffed.

I crossed my chest with my finger. "Cross my heart. I'll call Marcus Monday and tell him."

Marla showed up on time and introduced herself to the group. She was a short, heavyset woman with a broad smile and a kind expression. She wore proper shoes, had binoculars hanging from her neck, and carried a wooden walking stick.

"I've never birded, but I like to hike." She bumped the ground with her walking stick.

"I've never done either. But I'm ready to learn," Hazel said.

Shortie, familiar with NAS Pensacola and Fort Barrancas after his stint as an MP there, led the way. He wore khaki cargo shorts and a faded Journey T-shirt and scrutinized the area. On guard for bad guys, I assumed.

"Let's take this Woodland Nature Trail. It's a quarter mile." He checked his watch and pointed at my boot. "If we walked it, it would only be fifteen minutes maximum. Peg, will that be too much for you? It might take longer since we're looking for birds."

"I think I can do it. I'll stop if I need to."

"What kind of birds will we spot?" Owen had binoculars looped over his neck, and he wore a vest with multiple pockets, a small notebook and pens stuck in them.

"I brought the list Sylvia gave us." I waved my paper, and a pall fell over the original group. Hazel and Marla walked ahead of us.

Shortie lowered his voice and tipped his chin at the two women. "Does Marla know about Anna or Sylvia?"

"No, and I'd rather not tell her two of our original birders died within three days of each other."

"It still seems surreal." Carmen hunched her shoulders, and Owen gave her a side hug. "Sylvia was so strange, an oxymoron."

Her word choice hit the spot. Sylvia came across as a gentle person. No airs about her. But she lived alone in a huge, expensive house. And she'd been murdered.

Shortie leaned toward me. "Will Hazel spill the beans?"

"No, I asked her not to."

"You two seem to be getting along better."

"Sometimes I think so, and then she pulls a 'Hazel.'" I shrugged.

"Like I said, she wants attention. This group might be helpful. When is she going home?"

"Her roof needs replacing, according to her. You saw her house. What did you think?"

"It does. She'll need a total roof replacement. She called the insurance company right away. Are you going to let her stay at your house?"

"I have to. Plus, I kind of like CB."

"What about that bird?" he asked with a laugh.

I raised one eyebrow. Roscoe was the noisiest thing I've ever had in my house. Louder than Carter and his teenage buddies. And messier. He kicked seeds out and ensured most fell behind the buffet. The heavy buffet I couldn't move to vacuum behind.

Hazel turned and put a finger to her lips, waving us forward. She pointed. A small, yellowish bird with an olive-colored back and two white stripes on its gray wings sat on a branch in a pine tree.

"What is it?" Carmen asked.

Owen held up a finger. "I've been studying our list, and I think this is a pine warbler." He pulled a small birding book from one of his vest pockets and thumbed through it. "Yes, right here." He turned the book for us to see.

"Where did you get the list?" Marla asked.

"Sylvia gave it to them," Hazel said.

Marla tipped her head. "Who's that? She didn't come today?"

Oops, Hazel mouthed.

"WE NEED to add a disclosure on your flyer at the pool," Shortie said. Marla appeared shocked when we told her what happened to Anna and Sylvia but didn't seem to hold it against us.

I toed the dirt path. "I should take it down. Marla wasn't upset, but some people might be."

Hazel slowed and let the others walk ahead of us. She hooked her arm through Shortie's.

"Marla and I talked when we first started walking before my 'oops.' I'm sorry about that, Peg."

I waved off her apology.

"Anyhow, she knows Sylvia. She slipped and said that's how she heard about our group."

"But she told me she found the flyer at the pool. And she just asked who Sylvia was," I said.

"That's what caught my attention. I didn't say anything." She mimed zipping her lips.

Eyebrows furrowed, Shortie said, "Why would she say

Sylvia told her and then act surprised she died? If they were friends, wouldn't she already know? Something seems fishy."

"What do we do?"

"Keep an eye on her," he said. "She's moved up to a suspect for me."

Hazel tugged her notebook out of her crossbody tote and scribbled in it. "Now we have three suspects."

"Three?"

"Yes. Charlene, Marla, and the anonymous caller who threatened Peg." She tucked the notebook and pen back into her tote bag.

Shortie stopped short. "What?"

Hazel's head shot up. *Oops,* she mouthed. Again.

Chapter 10

If I wasn't still bruised and battered from my fall, Shortie might have strangled me. After Hazel's slip, he blinked several times and rubbed his hand over his jaw, scratching the raspy stubble. I opened my mouth.

He held up his hand, palm out. "Don't, Peg." He walked a few steps away and turned back. "How do you get yourself into these situations?"

I grimaced. I had no idea, so no answer for him. Silence was my friend right now.

"When did this happen?"

"Thursday night," I said.

"Have you told Sharp?"

I stared at the ground.

Hazel stepped between us. "She's afraid to. But she promised me she'll call him Monday."

Shortie pulled his cell phone out of his pocket. "How about we do that now?"

I put my hand on his and gestured up the path. "Can we do it after we leave here? If Marla is a potential suspect, we need to meet with Marcus and tell him what she said too."

"You can follow me to the police station when we leave."

I considered saluting him, but his glare stopped me. "Yes, we will."

The group planned to eat lunch together after our outing. Shortie suggested a restaurant on base or the café inside the National Naval Aviation Museum.

"I'm not sure the restaurant is open today." Marla took out her phone. "I'll double-check, but we'll probably have to go to the café."

That reminded me. Earlier, my cell buzzed in my pocket. I pulled it out to check and found a missed voicemail. I clicked to listen.

"Hi, this is Charlene Newman. I'm Sylvia Newman's daughter. I wondered if I could meet with you. Thanks." She left her number.

I pulled Shortie aside and handed him my phone. "Listen to the message. Charlene wants to see me. She's Sylvia's daughter."

Hazel joined us. "What's up?"

I filled her in while Shortie listened to Charlene's voicemail.

"What do you think?" I asked him.

He passed my cell back. "Sounds like a good idea. You have her on your suspect list?"

"Yes," Hazel said.

"Let's eat and then get together with her. Go ahead and set up a time for her to come by."

"To my house?" I asked.

He chewed on his lip. "No. Tell her the coffee shop on Nine Mile Road. But Peg? Then we're going to talk to Marcus."

I stepped away to return Charlene's call. I thanked her for calling and told her I was sorry about her mother's death. Then

I asked her to meet me in two hours, leaving out Shortie and Hazel would be with me.

The restaurant at the Naval Air Station we wanted to go to wasn't open for lunch on Saturdays, so we headed to the café instead. Located inside the National Naval Aviation Museum, it was a replica of the old bar area at the Cubi Point Officers' Club in the Philippines. Aviator squadron plaques from the original bar covered the walls, and the café was open to the museum. Their quesadilla was my favorite, and my stomach growled in happy anticipation.

Service was quick, and Shortie, Hazel, and I finished before the others. We said our goodbyes and hurried to our cars. My mother-in-law set her purse and binoculars in the passenger seat of the car.

"Can you move those?" I maneuvered around to get in with my bulky boot.

She smirked. "Why don't you ride with Shortie?"

"Why?" Something was up with my mother-in-law.

She gunned the engine and began to back up. "Catch him before he leaves, dear."

I closed the car door and shuffled out of the way. Shortie stood beside his Jeep.

"You need a ride?"

"Yeah. She wouldn't let me go with her."

"She's a matchmaker." He chuckled and helped me get up in his vehicle. I swung my booted leg around.

"She's a nut. Sorry about this."

He buckled up, then reached over and touched my hand. "Don't be sorry. We're friends, but I wondered ..."

My stomach, full of the quesadilla, now flip-flopped at his words. Curiosity filled me, but before he continued, my phone rang, showing "Private." My heart raced. "It's the caller. The mysterious caller."

His jaw clenched. "Answer it and put it on speaker."

I hit the accept and speaker buttons on my cell. "Hello?"

The caller's voice boomed. "You better listen and stay away. I'm not going to tell you again."

I clicked to end the call and dropped my phone on my lap. "That was it, Shortie. That person. Can you tell who it is? They ... they called me again. How did they find my number?" My words ended with a wail.

He wrapped his arms around me as best he could in the confines of the Jeep. "I've got you. We'll figure this out."

He held me for a minute and then sat back. I wiped my eyes and sniffled.

"No tissues, sorry."

"That's all right." I drew in a deep breath and slowly let it out. "I'm scared."

"I'm sure." His gray eyes, usually full of light and joy, were flat and hard. "Let's go. Then we're going to find Marcus." He put his hand on the back of my seat and backed out. Then he slid his hand over mine and squeezed it. I held on tight all the way to the coffee shop.

Tall and slim like her mother, Charlene sat at one of the outside patio tables. Hazel took the seat beside her, and I pulled up a chair while Shortie ordered us iced coffees.

I shoved my fear about the unknown caller aside and touched Charlene's shoulder. "I'm so sorry about your mother. You resemble her."

She gave a half smile, her face lined with grief. "I can't believe she's gone."

Hazel scooted her seat closer and hugged her. "It's hard to lose a parent." She brushed her hair off of her face. "And you're so young."

What was my mother-in-law up to? It wasn't normal for her to comfort someone.

"How did you find out about your mother?" She patted Charlene's arm and winked at me.

"The police showed up at my apartment. A Detective Sharp, I think? He told me." She frowned at me. "Did you find her?"

"Yes. I'm sorry it happened that way. I thought your mom was a kind person. And she loved birds."

She grimaced and rubbed her hands together. "She did. That's what caused all this trouble." Emotion filled her voice.

Shortie returned, handed out the drinks, and took the empty seat beside me. He introduced himself to Charlene and offered his condolences.

"Charlene said Sylvia's love for birds caused 'all this trouble.'" I made air quotes and turned back to her. "What did you mean?"

Her body stiffened. "I'm not sure I should talk about this."

Hazel dug into her purse and pulled out her notebook and pen. Flipping to a clean page, she clicked the pen and held it ready. "Have you informed the police? Why don't you tell us, dear? It'll help you feel better."

My mother-in-law—a master at getting people to talk.

"Well, when I was little, she took me birding with her."

I remembered Sylvia told us that the first night.

"And?" Hazel prompted, glancing up from her notes.

"We stopped when I hit my teens. Too busy, I guess. But a few years ago, Mom said she'd started birding again." Charlene picked at her flaming red nail polish. "And that she'd met someone."

We straightened up and glanced at each other.

Hazel continued her line of questioning. "Did you find out who?"

"Not for sure. She never introduced me to him, but I think he was married." Color rose on her neck and spotted her cheeks. She blinked back tears. "It wasn't the first time she'd had an affair with a married man."

Hazel scribbled everything she said. She put her pen down and passed Charlene a napkin. "No need to be embarrassed. It's not your fault."

She wiped her eyes and blotted her nose. In a whisper, she added, "My biological father was married when she had an affair with him."

Charlene's father and Sylvia's mystery boyfriend were now potential suspects. Hazel jotted names in a different part of her notebook.

"What's your father's name, dear?"

"Roger Keaton."

The three of us gasped in unison. Roger Keaton was a household name in Pensacola. Right up there with Emmitt Smith and Addison Russell. But not for good reasons. Keaton had been arrested numerous times—all for violent charges. Each time, someone died or disappeared, and he got off scot-free. His wife of forty years stood by his side throughout each ordeal.

"I can tell what you're thinking." Charlene's voice was harsh. She stood and smoothed her skirt. "My father isn't the killer. But the person my mom was seeing? That's who the police need to find. Leave my father alone. He's had enough problems." She picked up her purse and keys, turned on her heel, and left.

Hazel clicked her pen and slammed her notebook shut. "I don't care what she said. Roger Keaton is staying on my list. That man is trouble with a capital 'T.' The police need to know Sylvia's connection to him."

"We never got to ask how birding connected to Sylvia's death."

"Call her later. For now, let's go see Marcus." Shortie stood and threw our empty cups away.

My foot, ankle, and hip throbbed. My entire body was out of whack from my boot and shoe height difference, and my ankle was puffy. Dragging the boot around all day was hard work. Shortie called Marcus and asked him to come by my house when he could, and we all headed to the parking lot. I stopped at Hazel's car and climbed in when she unlocked the door.

"Thanks for letting me ride in the Bug. No way I could manage to climb back up in the Jeep."

"Shortie would've been happy to help you."

My mother-in-law had her heart set on my having a boyfriend. I bit back the harsh words that sprang to my lips and reminded myself she meant well.

At home, I swallowed a couple of ibuprofen, and stretched out on the couch. Never a fan of pain pills, I'd thrown away the last few in the prescription bottle and changed to over-the-counter pain relievers the day before. Shortie turned off the overhead lights and closed the sliding door blinds. He set a lightweight blanket over Roscoe's cage so the bird would sleep.

"Get some rest, Peg. Hazel and I will sit at the table until Marcus gets here. He said it'll be another hour or so before he can come." He patted his leg, and CB followed him to the table, groaning when he lay on the floor—Charlie Brown, the drama king, just like his mistress.

Hazel tucked a pillow under my ankle and whispered, "How fun is this? Two handsome men in your house."

I groaned from the pain and her words. Shortie might call her a matchmaker, but my mother-in-law was, in Zack's famous words, a 'buttinsky.'"

The two whispered, which faded into the background. Exhaustion caught up with me, and I fell asleep in minutes. CB barked what I thought was seconds later. Marcus had arrived. I pushed myself up to sit and swiped my hand over my face. Brushing my teeth and hair would help. I shuffled my way into the bathroom before he came inside.

I found Hazel, Shortie, and Marcus seated at my dining table. Stalling for time, I poured myself a glass of sweet tea. Shortie jumped up and carried it to the table for me. I followed him and sat opposite Marcus, keeping my gaze on my glass.

He cleared his throat. "Peg?"

"Hi."

The muscle in his jaw twitched. "How are you?"

"Fine, I'm fine. How are you?"

"Good. It's good to see you," he deadpanned.

"You too."

Hazel and Shortie watched us like spectators at a tennis match. One that threatened to erupt into angry words.

Marcus spread his hands wide. "So, I came here today for … what?"

Hazel jumped right in, opening her notebook and thrusting it toward him. "This is our list of suspects in Sylvia's case." She pointed and ran her finger down the list. "Charlene, she's Sylvia's daughter, and her father is Roger Keaton. You know all about him, I'm sure."

He answered with a slight lift of his eyebrows.

"Today, we went birding, and a new person joined us. Marla. She said she knew Sylvia and then pretended she didn't. What's her last name?" She turned to me.

"Not sure. She never mentioned it."

"Well. So Marla, Charlene, and Roger Keaton. And Charlene said her mother was seeing someone. A married man, she thought."

Shortie cleared his throat.

"Yeah, and Peg's anonymous caller." Hazel closed her

notebook. She held up five fingers. "We have five suspects. How many do the police have?"

"Anonymous caller?" Marcus glared. His dimples appeared, but not because he was smiling. He ground his teeth.

"Yeah." I stretched out the word. "Someone called me."

"Twice," Shortie added.

I held up my hand. "Twice. I should have informed you when the first call came. It happened two days ago, and then the person called again today."

He shifted his focus to Shortie. "Did you hear it?"

"Yep, I did today. Couldn't tell if it was a man or woman, but Peg said it was the same voice as the other one she received."

"It was. But it's disguised. And they said the same thing both times: that I should stay away."

Marcus exhaled through his nose. "That might be the best idea, don't you think?"

Chapter 11

Marcus had a point, but he wasn't the one who got the phone calls. I was scared and wanted to find out who murdered Sylvia. Now I had a dog in the fight, and I wouldn't back down. He didn't have to understand my motive. I motioned for Hazel to slide her notebook to me and flipped to her list, running my finger down the names.

"Has your department checked out Charlene? Or Roger Keaton? Did y'all know Sylvia had a boyfriend?"

Marcus shoved his chair back and stood. CB sat up and woofed, and Marcus leaned over and patted the dog's head. "Yes, no, and yes. We talked to Charlene. I'm sure she told you. I was uninformed about Keaton being her father. We found a number on Ms. Newman's cell we suspected was a boyfriend from the texts we read. It was a burner phone, or he blocked the number."

Hazel rubbed her hands together and wiggled in her seat. "Oh, a burner phone! Isn't this fun?" She quivered with excitement.

I gave her the stink eye, and she settled down.

"Sorry." She tucked her hands under her legs. "I got carried away."

Marcus headed for the front door.

"Hang on, what about Marla?" I asked.

He turned, his hand on the doorknob. "Tell me again why you think she's a suspect?"

"She told me she found my notice on the bulletin board at the UWF pool. But when she talked to Hazel, she said Sylvia told her about our group. Then she asked who Sylvia was when we mentioned her."

Marcus pursed his lips, thinking. "Find out her last name, will you? And Peg, tomorrow. The station." He pulled the door tight behind him.

Shortie refused Hazel's offer of dinner and left. I wasn't sure what we would eat, but I wouldn't be cooking. My foot and leg still ached, and I settled on the couch, rehearsing my statement for tomorrow.

Hazel perched on the edge of the coffee table, still flushed with excitement. "I have an idea."

I opened one eye. "What?"

"We can ask Marla what her last name is." She leaned over and grabbed my cell phone, thrusting it at me. "Tell her we're making a roster of contact information."

I took my cell and laid it on my stomach. "Then we have to make the roster."

"Yep. So, ask her."

I offered the phone to her. "You do it. You can be the birding group secretary."

"I've never been a secretary before." Her eyes lit up.

"Might as well make the rounds and write down

everyone's information. It'll be helpful to have it. I'm going to rest for a bit." I yawned.

"Got it. I'll go to my room so I don't disturb you." She called CB, and he trotted after her.

Next thing I knew, Hazel was shaking my arm. "Wake up, Peg. I have news."

I pushed myself up. The blinds to the back deck stood open, and it was dark outside.

"What time is it?"

"It's after nine. But, listen. I talked to everyone and got their information. Guess who Marla is married to?"

I stood and stretched. "Who?"

"The mayor." She smirked.

"What mayor?"

"Pensacola's, Neil Braden. Marla is Braden's wife. Guess what that means?"

"I'm not awake enough for guessing games." I hobbled to the kitchen. "Did you make dinner?"

She followed me and perched on a bar stool. "I didn't want to wake you. No more guessing games. You may not know, but our illustrious city leader has a history of affairs."

I got the carton of eggs and a loaf of bread out of the refrigerator. "We'll have breakfast for dinner."

"Did you hear what I said?"

"Yes. What does that have to do with anything?" I reached into a cabinet for my favorite skillet and set it on the stove. "How many eggs do you want?"

Hazel held up two fingers and kept talking. "What if Sylvia had an affair with him?"

I cracked eggs into the skillet, adding a little salt and pepper. "How did you get to that conclusion?" I turned toward her, pointing with the spatula. "That's a big jump."

"I agree, but it's a possibility. Everyone who's anyone knows he's like that. No idea why Marla stays with him."

"I didn't know."

She raised an eyebrow. "Anyhow, when I called Marla, I asked her where she met Sylvia. I reminded her she'd mentioned she had told her about our birding group."

It didn't escape me she said "our" birding group. "And?"

"She backtracked. Said she meant someone else." Hazel got out two plates and took butter and jelly from the refrigerator, setting them on the table. "So then I asked her where she was when Sylvia was killed."

I was sliding eggs onto the plates and almost dropped the skillet. "You did what? Hazel! What in the world?" I set the pan down, added toast to each plate, and carried them to the table. "You need to be careful."

She sat and bowed her head. "Pray, please."

After praying, I touched her arm. "Really, you do need to be careful."

"I acted clueless. Which is true." She took a bite, chewed, and swallowed. "I wasn't there when Sylvia died, so it wasn't a lie."

I huffed and made a face. "You're kind of sneaky."

"Yep."

HAZEL'S DISCOVERY ran through my mind all night. Early Sunday morning, I headed to the local police department, gave my statement—short and sweet—and was fingerprinted. The process was quick, and I thought Marcus had passed the word to be nice to me. Who would've thought he'd watch out for me?

"That was quick," Hazel said when I got home.

"It wasn't too awful." I scrunched my nose. "Marcus wasn't there, and the female police officer who took my statement was nice."

She raised an eyebrow. "Didn't treat you like a suspect, huh?"

"Right."

Hazel helped me strip the beds and cleaned the hall bathroom while I wiped down mine. Vacuuming with my boot was impossible, and I didn't want to ask my mother-in-law, so I called Lauree.

"Hey there," she said. "Haven't talked to you in a few days."

"I'm sorry. And I have a favor to ask."

"What's up?"

"Could you vacuum for me?"

"Sure, I'll be over in a few."

She hugged me when she came in. "I've missed you! How are you?" She pointed at my foot. "When do you go for a checkup?"

"Not for a couple of weeks. I appreciate you helping me today. Hazel cleaned her bathroom and did laundry, but this would be hard on her back."

"No problem." She headed to the laundry room and retrieved the vacuum. It didn't take her long to go over the living room, my room, and Hazel's room. She wrapped up the cord when she finished and stuck it all back in its space.

"Thank you. No need to do the other rooms when we haven't been in them."

"Nope, I agree." She grabbed a glass of ice water band joined me on the couch. "Where is Hazel?"

"She took CB to the doggie park."

She tipped her chin toward Roscoe. "How's the bird?"

He piped up, "Who's the bird? Who's the bird?"

"He's been fine. He's noisy, but I'm used to it now. Want an update on the murders?" I grabbed a couch pillow, hugging it to my chest.

"Yes." Lauree set her glass down and settled back on the sofa.

"Maybe you can help me make sense of all this too. And, fair warning, I got a mysterious, threatening phone call." I held up my hand at her expression. "Yes, the police have been informed. When I got the second one, Shortie was with me, and he heard it."

She grabbed my hand. "Ever since you created this birding group, it's been one disaster after another."

"None of this was what I'd planned," I said. Helping my empty nest problems had just created more issues.

"I know, I'll reserve judgment. Tell me everything."

I gave the short version of the last few days. Lauree winced several times.

"Do I have this straight?" she asked when I finished. She counted down on each finger. "Potential suspects are Charlene; her father Roger Keaton, the worst criminal in Pensacola, by the way; Marla Braden, the mayor's wife; and Sylvia's unknown married boyfriend." Her eyebrows were so high they disappeared under her bangs.

"And my mysterious caller."

"What did he say?"

"I couldn't tell if it was a man or woman. Shortie couldn't, either. Whoever it was told me to stay away. That's all they said."

"You, my friend, have gotten yourself into a pickle."

∼

Lauree invited me for dinner, and I left Hazel a note on the dining table before I went over. The twins answered my knock and led me to the kitchen.

Stevie's face scrunched up with concern. "What happened to your leg?"

"I fell and fractured my ankle."

Suzie hugged me. "Does it hurt?"

I brushed her hair back. "No, honey. It's not bad. What are we having for dinner?" I needed to distract them before they started poking at my boot.

"P'sgetti." Her lisp made me smile.

"Spaghetti, Suze, remember?" As the oldest twin by mere minutes, Stevie enjoyed bossing her.

She stuck her tongue out at him.

"All right, you two. Quit and go set the table." Lauree motioned to me with the noodle spoon. "Take a seat. John will be back soon. He went to his brother's house to watch the University of Florida and Florida State football game."

I grinned. "Who won?"

"No idea."

"Me neither, but when he comes in, I'll be sure to say, 'Go Gators.' He sure doesn't like them."

Suzie set a napkin at my place. "Daddy went to Florida State."

"Yes, he did. That's why I tease him. UF and Florida State are rivals."

"Yes! Daddy said next year, I can go see them play," Stevie exclaimed.

"I don't like football." Suzie pulled her chair out and sat beside me, chin in her hand. "It's boring." She stretched the word out into three syllables.

My feelings mirrored hers, but John was a huge fan, and I

didn't want to discourage his daughter. "There's food at the game. That's fun, right?"

She nodded her agreement like a bobble-head toy. Lauree passed bowls of spaghetti around and set a plate of toasted garlic bread in the middle of the table.

We held hands, bowed our heads, and Lauree prayed, then she passed me the bread. "We won't wait on John. He'll be home later."

Dinner was yummy, and the twins kept us laughing. After we finished, I volunteered to help Lauree clean up the dishes.

"I wanted to talk to you about something else." I handed her the rinsed silverware.

"Okay ..." She placed the silverware in the dishwasher and took a plate from me. "What's up? I thought you already gave me all the juicy deets."

I turned off the sink and dried my hands on the kitchen towel. "I realized I don't have as much time for the blog. Would you be interested in taking on more of it?"

Surprise dawned on her face before a smile took over. "Um, sure. Yes, actually, I would." She reached for the towel, wiped her hands, and hung it to dry. "I've been thinking of some ideas for posts and all."

I hugged her. "Perfect, thank you. And you'll get a raise too."

She wiggled her eyebrows and did a little dance. "Whoo hoo!"

I told her and the kids goodnight and headed home. When I opened the front door, my cell phone rang, and I hurried to answer it.

"You don't know who you're messing with if Marla Braden is in your birding group."

I plopped onto a chair at the dining table. "Marcus?"

"Yes." In a monotone voice, he said, "Peg, I am worried you're in over your head."

"What do you mean?"

Noises in the background came through the line, and then footsteps, followed by quiet. "Listen, you don't want to mess with the Bradens."

He was warning me? Why? "Are you trying to tell me something?"

"Yes," he hissed. "I can't be specific. You have to trust me. You trust me, don't you?"

"I do, but I don't understand."

He huffed. "Can I come over?"

"Um, sure."

"See you in five."

Marcus hung up, and I stared at the table. I had no idea what was going on, but I didn't like it. A noise behind me made me jump, and my heart raced.

I grabbed the back of the chair and turned. "Hazel!"

"Hmm?" Her head jutted forward like a turtle. "What's the matter?"

My hand on my chest, I exhaled. "You startled me, that's all. I didn't know y'all were back." CB trotted to my side and nuzzled my hand until I scratched his head.

"Who was that?"

"Marcus. He's coming by."

"Oh! You are going to have a gentleman caller."

"No, nothing like that." I sat at the table and rubbed my face. "He seems to think Marla is trouble. He warned me away from her."

She pulled a chair out and sat, lips pursed. "That's strange."

"Mm-hmm." I tapped my phone to check the time. "He should be here any minute."

Chapter 12

I waited for Marcus in the old rocker on the front porch, legs stretched out, and my good foot rested on top of my boot. The sun was setting, and the sky burned with golds and tans. A gentle pine-scented breeze wafted by. My shoulders relaxed, and I reminded myself God was always in control. He knew all the details.

Marcus parked at the curb instead of my crazy, steep driveway. He trudged down the sloped yard and sat on a porch step, where we stayed in silence for several seconds before he cleared his throat and said, "I'm not here, and I haven't told you this."

I cocked an eyebrow. "Okay, this is secret spy stuff."

"Marla can remain in your birding group, but she is not, and won't be, part of the investigation of Sylvia's death. Tell Shortie and your mother-in-law." He patted his knees and stood. "You shouldn't be investigating this anyhow. I'm the detective."

"Obey you, you mean." It wasn't a question. I wanted to cross my arms, stick my tongue out, and say, 'You're not the boss of me!'

He turned and stepped up onto the porch. I stood and faced him. In the dim porch light, his brown eyes were almost black. I reached out and traced his dimple with my finger.

Marcus sighed. "Peg, please." He took my hand and squeezed it. "I want you to be careful. You don't understand who you're messing with."

"I have a slight idea. With Roger Keaton in the mix, I know there can be trouble."

He turned and stepped off the porch. He lifted his hand, and as he walked away, he muttered, "Keaton is the least of your worries."

Hazel waited for me on the other side of the front door.

"What did he say? I tried to listen through the door but couldn't make it all out." She was like CB when he got a bone—excited and impossible to calm down.

I ran my hands through my hair. "That man! He makes me nuts." I ground out the last word.

She sat beside me, patting my hand. "You like him. I'm okay with that. Zack has been gone a long time."

"What?"

"You like him. He likes you," she singsonged.

"This was nothing about that." My finger, the one that traced his dimple, tingled, and I shoved my hand under my leg. "He warned me—no, he commanded me—to avoid Marla. She can stay in the birding group but won't be part of the investigation."

"Why?"

"No idea. He said I didn't know who I was messing with. I assumed he meant Roger Keaton. But, then he said Keaton was the least of my worries. And that I don't need to investigate. He can do it all."

"Today I found out the mayor is going to run for a senate seat."

Her subject change startled me. "Oh? What's that got to do with anything?

"Everything, Peg."

She hurried off and returned with the notebook. "I think it creates some motive." She handed the notebook and a pen to me. "What are you thinking?"

I turned to a fresh page and wrote down the left side:

- Charlene
- Roger Keaton
- Marla Braden & Neil Braden
- Anonymous caller
- Sylvia's boyfriend

Then I drew a line through the Bradens' names. Marcus had forbidden me to investigate Marla, and I assumed that meant her husband too.

"Add that Neil Braden is running for a senate seat," Hazel said.

I did, and we stared at the list. I tapped my pen on the last name.

"We need to find out who Sylvia was seeing."

We sat in silence until she yelled, "I got it!"

CB barked and ran around the living room. Roscoe chirped, "I'm the bird, I'm the bird," and I almost fell out of my seat.

"You've got what?" At this rate, her enthusiasm would be the death of me.

She snapped her fingers, raced to her room, and returned with a packet of envelopes. Dropping them on the table, she pointed. "Remember? I found them in Sylvia's purse, shoved them in my bag, and forgot about them."

"I'm sure they're just bills."

"Nope." She pushed the bundle toward me. "Here. I never opened them, but one thing I did notice is they are hand-addressed. No return address. They're not bills." Her eyes gleamed with self-importance. All that was left was for her to blow on her knuckles and rub them on her chest.

She jutted her head forward. "Well?"

"Oh, sorry." My daydream about her distracted me. Fanning through the letters, I realized what she said was true. I took off the rubber band and counted them. "Twelve. There are twelve envelopes."

"Well, let's open them."

I spread them on the table, and we put them in order by the date mailed. Four envelopes were blank, each stuffed with several sheets of paper.

"Are those dated?" I pointed to the blank ones.

She picked one up and opened it, her eyes growing wider as she read. "This is an email, Peg. You won't believe who this is from."

"Who?"

She opened the other three, scanning each. "All four are emails between Sylvia and the mayor."

"Braden?"

"Yeah."

Wow, I mouthed. We'd found a direct link between Sylvia and Neil Braden.

"Wonder who these others are from?"

Hazel picked up the earliest dated one and pulled out a card. She read it and paled.

"What is it? What's wrong?"

She dropped the card, and her voice quivered when she said, "This is from Marla. She threatened to kill Sylvia."

~

Marcus warned me away from Marla, but I had proof of a relationship between her, her husband, and Sylvia. Plus, her written warning to Sylvia. What should I do next?

"What do we do?" Hazel's words were an eerie reflection of my thoughts.

"Let's open the other envelopes before we play guessing games."

When we finished, we had a stack of eight cards from Marla, all with the same basic threat.

"You think she kept these as proof?" Hazel asked.

"Sylvia?"

"Yeah." Hazel's eyes reddened, and a single tear ran down her cheek. "She must have thought something would happen."

"This is getting more and more complicated."

"Let's finish." Dejection rang through her voice.

We still had to read the emails, so I picked up the first one and read aloud.

"My dearest Sylvia, I cannot wait until we see each other again. I am so glad you enjoyed our trip to Santa Fe. Our nights together fill my mind. I know you're worried Marla will find out about us, but trust me, she's not a problem. She stays with me, but she doesn't care about me anymore than I do her. You, my dear Sylvia, are my love. My heart. Till we are together again, Neil."

I grimaced and dropped the paper. "Yuck."

"Yes, yuck." Hazel pointed at the bottom of the page I'd read. "What does that say?"

I leaned closer and read Sylvia's response. "Oh, this is what she said back to him." I cleared my throat. "Dearest Neil, I loved our time away from Pensacola. How fun that you snuck me into your hotel! I hate you had to work while we were in Santa Fe, but our nights were magical. I'm not afraid of Marla. I just want to be with you. With love, Sylvia."

I made a gagging face, and Hazel giggled.

"Hand me the emails. And let's put these in order by date," Hazel said. "That way, we can find out when Marla mailed her cards. Like, did she find her husband's emails and then threaten Sylvia?"

"She must have."

She clicked her pen and scribbled on the envelopes. "I'm going to date the front of these blanks with the dates on the emails." She held up one. "This one is the first. It's dated the fourth of July."

Two of the emails were dated back-to-back, then two cards from Marla, followed by another email, three cards from Marla, the last email, and then three more cards.

Hazel waved her hand over the table. "This is crazy. How did Marla discover the affair?"

"And why did Sylvia and Neil continue it when Sylvia received the threatening letters?"

She rubbed her chin. "Maybe she didn't tell Neil."

"You think? We better read these emails and see if she says anything in them." My hand hovered over them. "I'm almost afraid to read these. Besides the gag factor, I'm wondering if we should turn these over to Marcus. I hate to do it, though. He's already said the Bradens won't be investigated."

Hazel shook one of Marla's letters. "Even with proof? Didn't he only mention Marla?"

"Hmm, you're right. We could compare the handwriting on the letters to something Marla has written?"

"You don't think it's Marla's?"

"The police won't investigate Marla, and I don't know why. So, if I give these to Marcus, the police might stuff them in a file somewhere."

"You think he's crooked? I thought you liked him."

"Marcus? I do. Like him, I mean."

She beamed and pumped her fist in the air. "I knew it!"

I held up my hand. "Hang on. I don't think he's crooked. But I don't know who told him Marla wouldn't be investigated. We have to assume that means her husband too. My impression was it didn't come from Marcus. So, we have to prove beyond a shadow of a doubt Marla wrote these."

She sat back and crossed her arms. "I see what you mean. Time to schedule another birding outing and somehow get Marla to write something."

"Yep." I examined my list in her notebook. "So, Neil Braden was the married man Sylvia was seeing." I added his name to the list beside number five.

1. Charlene
2. Roger Keaton
3. ~~Marla Braden & Neil Braden/running for a senate seat~~
4. Anonymous caller
5. Sylvia's boyfriend – Neil Braden

Then I circled number four—the anonymous caller—and tapped my pen on the paper. "This is what we need to figure out next. We shouldn't rule out Roger Keaton, either."

"You think Marla is the caller?"

She obviously had a reason to hate Sylvia. But murder her? I shrugged. "I'm not sure. None of this makes sense to me."

"Why don't you call Shortie? Another pair of eyes on all this will help."

I picked up my phone to text him and realized how late it was. "I'll text him about meeting us tomorrow. I don't want to wake him."

Hazel nodded, let CB out front to potty, and got Roscoe some fresh feed. I opened the blinds across the sliding glass doors, flipped the back porch light on, and glared at the offending tree still lying across my deck. Hazel finished her pet chores and joined me.

"Has insurance said when they'll do something about this?"

"Nope. Any word on your roof?"

She grunted. "No, nothing yet." She hooked her arm through mine and laid her head on my shoulder. "We'll get through this, Peg, I promise."

I hugged her arm to my side. My irritating mother-in-law was becoming my friend.

Who woulda thunk it?

Chapter 13

Shortie waited at an outside table when Hazel and I pulled up to the coffee shop. She volunteered to buy my coffee and a slice of lemon pound cake while I hobbled to the chair across from him.

"You're getting around better," he said, pointing to my boot.

I tapped my tennis shoe on the ground. "This shoe is the right height for the boot, so I'm much more comfortable. By the end of the day, though, I'm ready to sit."

"I'm sure." His eyes lit up, and he reached for my hand. "I wanted to ask you something."

Hazel plopped into the seat between us before I could take his hand. Shortie sat back with a grimace.

"I'll wait out here for our order." Hazel dug into her purse and set her notebook on the wrought iron table. "Have you filled him in yet?"

"Not yet." This made the second time he wanted to ask me something, and we were interrupted. I couldn't decide how I felt about it. I assumed he was going to invite me on a date, and I kind of liked the idea. Then Marcus's face flashed through my mind—those dimples.

Ugh, I'm too old for this.

She flipped to the list we had written the night before. "We narrowed our suspects down."

Shortie's lips twitched. "You did?"

"Yes." She pushed the notebook closer to him and read off the names.

"Why is there a line across Marla's name?" Shortie asked.

"Marcus told Peg they won't be investigating her."

His brows furrowed.

Hazel held a finger up. "Hang on. I think that's our order. Be right back." She bustled into the coffee shop. The aroma of freshly brewed coffee drifted out, and my mouth watered.

Shortie crossed his arms over his chest. "I'm confused. Marcus said they won't investigate Marla?" He reached out and tapped the notebook. "And you think Sylvia's unknown boyfriend is the mayor?"

"We have proof. While we have a Hazel-free minute, what did you want to ask me?"

"Let's wait until we have more than a minute."

Disappointment shot through me, but I agreed with him. Besides, I needed to consider if I wanted more than a friendship with him or Marcus—dimples or not. As Hazel had said, Zack had been gone for years. But I had to make a conscious decision to date someone. I'd never thought about it before while I was raising the kids.

Hazel returned with our coffees and my pound cake. She sat and pulled her notebook closer. "Did Peg tell you we have emails between the mayor and Sylvia?"

"No. How did you get those?"

"Well ..." I began.

She patted my arm. "Let me tell him, dear." She

straightened up in her chair, raised her chin, stared him down, and recapped what we had discovered so far.

He leaned back, a confused expression on his face. "What did the emails and letters say?"

"Marla threatened to kill Sylvia." I'd all but crumbled my pound cake into tiny pieces. I pinched some of the smaller crumbs together and popped them into my mouth, savoring the lemon deliciousness.

It took a minute for him to respond. When he did, his voice was gruff. "What did you say?"

I swallowed, sipped my coffee to chase the cake, and cleared my throat. "She said she would kill Sylvia for having an affair with her husband."

He shoved his chair back, stood, and closed his eyes.

"Shortie?" Hazel reached for his hand, but he jerked away.

His jaw clenched, and his shoulders rose. He stretched his neck side to side, shook his hands out, and exhaled. He glared at me. "Do you realize what you did was dangerous? All of this you've done."

"Yes."

"So, Marcus is aware of everything." He wasn't asking.

"Yes, but not about the letters or emails. Not yet."

Hazel batted her eyelashes. "We wanted your input before we talked to him."

"I'm not sure what to tell you." He rubbed his face, then moved his chair and sat. "Let me see if I have this straight." He held up his hand and counted down on his fingers, pinky first. "You broke into Sylvia's?"

Hazel raised her hand. "That was me. I learned how to from a movie."

He raised one eyebrow before lowering his ring finger. "And you found the receipt, which Marcus has."

I nodded once.

Middle finger—"And you have letters and emails he doesn't know about."

"Yes."

"Marcus said they won't investigate Marla." Pointer finger down. Last, his thumb went down. "And Sylvia had an affair with Neil Braden, our mayor."

"Yes." I opened my mouth to say more.

He stopped me with a raised hand. "You want to find out who the anonymous caller is. You think that's the killer?"

Hazel jumped in. "I think the caller is Marla, and she's the killer."

"But you have no proof."

I pointed to the notebook. "We have the letters she sent to Sylvia. Who else could it be?"

He tapped his finger on the list of names. "Roger Keaton?"

"Motive?" Hazel cocked an eyebrow and sat back, arms crossed.

"I don't know his motive, but he's a likelier candidate than the mayor or his wife. Both of whom are public figures." He clicked his tongue. "Plus, I don't see Marla Braden killing Sylvia."

"Why?" she asked.

"It's sexist, I guess. Just doesn't seem like she would."

I frowned. "That doesn't even make sense. You never saw women commit crimes when you were an MP?"

"Well, yeah, but ..."

Hazel cleared her throat and pushed her notebook back to Shortie. "Let's talk motives."

"Good idea. We're not here to argue, and I think you've told me all your secrets." His brow furrowed. "Right?"

"Sure." For now, anyhow.

Hazel pulled the notebook back, rummaged in her purse

for a pen, and wrote each person's name under a column headed 'Motives.'

"I don't think Charlene has a clear reason to kill her mother." Shortie sipped his coffee. "But not because she's a woman."

Hazel put a question mark in the motive column for Sylvia's daughter. "She didn't say anything that indicated she was mad enough at her mother to kill her."

"Could a daughter kill her mother? Stab her?" I shivered and wrapped my arms around myself.

"But she did mention Sylvia's love for birds caused all the trouble, remember?" she asked.

"I forgot about that. How in the world could loving birds get someone killed?"

"We can circle back to that." Shortie pointed to Roger Keaton's name. "He is a criminal for sure, but what's his motive for killing Sylvia?"

"Hazel, put a note by his name that we need to check on Sylvia's life insurance. I'm not saying he would kill her for that. Isn't he wealthy?" I shifted my boot to a more comfortable position.

"He has connections, but who knows about his finances," Shortie said.

"Life insurance might be a motive for either Charlene or her father," I added.

Hazel circled the Bradens' names. "So it all comes down to Marla and Neil."

"Whom Marcus told me wouldn't be a part of any of this."

Shortie tapped the notebook. "We need to find out why and do some more investigating." He glared at Hazel and then at me with a fierce expression. "But it needs to be legal. Got it?"

Hazel stuck her hand out for him to shake. "Of course."

I huffed. No way to promise that. Not with my mother-in-law by my side.

~

We split up the investigating chores—Hazel and I picked Marla, while Shortie took Roger Keaton. Mayor Neil Braden was a question mark. Although he had an affair with Sylvia, we didn't see a clear motive for him to kill her. Charlene was shelved for the moment.

"How will we check out Marla's story?" Hazel asked as she drove us home.

"I'm not sure, but there are two specific things we need to find out—why she denied knowing Sylvia and if she wrote those threatening cards."

She parked in my garage and turned to me. "Let's ask her over for coffee or lunch."

"We have to let Shortie in on our plans."

She followed me into the house. "Do you know any handwriting experts?"

A chuckle burst out of me, and Hazel chortled, complete with a snort. By the time we finished giggling, we had collapsed on the couch.

I held my belly. "Oh, that felt good."

"Sure did." She hiccupped. "Investigating murders is hard."

Her statement stopped our humorous moment in its track. "It's also sad," I said.

My phone, still tucked inside my purse, rang, and I pushed myself off the couch. "It's Chloe," I said, answering the call and hitting the speaker button.

"Hi, honey."

"Mom, are you sitting down?"

I pulled a bar stool up and sat. "I am now." My heart pounded, and my mouth was dry. "Are you okay?"

"I am." She whispered to Tom.

"What's going on? You're scaring me. Why is Tom home?"

"Don't be scared, Mom. Everything is fine. I wanted to ask you what you'd be doing in about eight months."

"Eight months?" Goosebumps slid along the back of my neck. "Eight months?"

Hazel sat up. *Is she pregnant?* she mouthed.

My mouth dropped open, and my grip on the phone tightened. "Chloe, are you ... are you pregnant?"

My daughter giggled. "Yes!"

"She is, Hazel, she is." Heat flushed my body, and joy filled my heart—a *baby*. My baby was having a baby. I shuffled off the bar stool and did an awkward happy dance.

Hazel sprang up from the couch and yelled, "Whoo hoo!" CB barked and zoomed through the dining and living room, and Roscoe piped up with, "Pretty bird, pretty bird."

When my house calmed down, I asked Chloe, "When are you due? When did you find out?"

"We went to the doctor today. I'm due late May or early June."

"I'm so happy for you both." I sniffled and wiped tears from my cheeks. "How are you feeling?"

"Morning sickness so far. But that just started."

"And the doctor said you're healthy?"

"Yes, Mom. I promise."

"This is so amazing. Your dad would be thrilled. He'd be a wonderful grandpa."

Chloe's voice was husky when she answered. "I know he would."

"I love you, honey. Tell Tom congratulations from Grandma Hazel and me. We need to meet for coffee soon."

Hazel leaned over my phone. "And shop for baby things!"

"Grandma Hazel is excited too." I chuckled.

Chloe laughed. "I can tell. I can't wait to shop!"

I hung up. "I'm going to be a grandma," I whispered.

"And I'll be a great-grandma," she whispered back.

We broke out in giggles again. I picked up my phone and searched for Marla's number. "We have to solve this mystery now—we have grandkid stuff to do."

I INVITED Marla to come for coffee the next morning, then texted Shortie and asked how things were going for him.

> I asked around about Keaton. Nothing new anyone could tell me. But I'll keep looking.

> Hmm. I invited Marla for coffee tomorrow.

> Where?

> My house. Hazel will be here.

> She may know how to jimmy a door open. Not sure about defending you.

> I think I'll be fine. CB will be here too.

> Text me when she arrives. Please.

I sent him a thumbs-up emoji, his concern for our safety making me feel warm and cared for. Marla wouldn't be a problem. At least I didn't think so.

Chapter 14

Early the next morning, I picked up a variety box of donuts, cherry scones, and blueberry muffins, plus a fruit tray from the grocery store. I set the sweets on a cut-glass plate and rearranged the fruit tray on a platter, then placed it all on the dining table, adding three small sandwich plates. The coffee was starting when Marla knocked on the front door.

Hazel answered it while I took three mugs out of the cabinet. My coffee cup collection was expansive and colorful. All my kids and friends knew gifting me a unique mug made me happy. I wanted to find a way to display them, but for now, they were stuffed in two of my largest kitchen cabinets.

Marla walked in, and I gestured to the dining table. "Hey, how are you? Sit wherever you want."

She inhaled. "It smells good in here."

"I found a fall blend in the coffee section at the grocery store, so that's brewing. Hazel, will you grab some creamer out of the fridge?" I carried a container of sugar and artificial sweeteners to the table and examined everything. "What else do we need?"

"Napkins," Marla and Hazel said at the same time, and we all chuckled.

"Definitely need those." I grabbed them and two mugs of coffee, handed it all out, and went back for the third cup—my favorite, showing a black cat with a bird sitting on his head.

"Thanks for inviting me this morning." Marla sipped her coffee. "Mmm, this is yummy."

I sniffed mine. "It makes it feel like fall." I pushed the treats toward her. "Help yourself."

We chose our snacks, and Hazel picked up the conversation baton. "So, Marla, you said you knew Sylvia?"

She had jumped right in with both feet. I stuffed part of my blueberry muffin in my mouth and waited for Marla's answer.

She wiped her lips and picked at the crumbs on her plate. "I sort of lied."

"Oh?" Hazel leaned closer.

"I said I saw the information about the birding group on the board at UWF. And I said Sylvia told me." She mushed the crumbs together and stuck them in her mouth. Her hand trembled as she lifted her coffee cup and sipped.

Hazel touched her arm. "Yes, you did. What really happened?"

Would she confess? Would this end today?

Marla sighed, her shoulders slumping. "So, I know, um, knew Sylvia. I overheard her tell someone about the birding group."

"Were you friends?"

Marla squirmed in her chair. "No. Not anymore."

Hazel and I stared at each other. If my expression resembled hers, it was deer in the headlights.

What now? Hazel mouthed.

I had no idea.

"Here's the truth. Sylvia had an affair with my husband."

Marla placed her napkin beside her plate. Tears welled and trickled down her cheeks. "I found out and sent her threatening letters. If the police find them ..." She dabbed at her eyes with her ring fingers.

"And?"

"Wouldn't you be mad if you found out someone was sleeping with your husband? And he's the mayor. How could she do that?" Her voice ended on a shrill note.

Roscoe piped up, "He's the mayor, he's the mayor!"

"I didn't know he had any vocabulary besides 'pretty bird,' 'who's the bird,' and 'I'm the bird,'" I said, chuckling.

"He knows all kinds of words," Hazel said. "He used to have a potty mouth, but I trained that out of him."

All I could think of was a potty beak instead of a potty mouth, and I snorted with laughter. Roscoe had distracted us from our mission. I rearranged my expression to convey sympathy, reached across the table, and patted Marla's hand. "I'm so sorry that happened."

"I am too. Sylvia and I were friends for years."

"That's awful. How did you find out?" Hazel asked.

"I ran across some emails between them. They were somewhat ... graphic." Her top lip curled.

My mind replayed what I'd read. "Have the police called? Did they find your letters?"

"No. Not yet." She set her mug down with a thunk, scooted her chair back, and stood. "I need to go."

"Don't rush off." Hazel blocked Marla's exit. "We don't have to talk about that."

Marla stepped around Hazel. "No, no, it's time I leave. Thank you for inviting me."

I jumped up and grabbed her arm. "Before you go, will you write down your address and birthday for our birding group information?"

Hazel shoved a pen and her notebook at her.

Marla leaned away from us. "What?"

"Jot it down before you leave. We're creating a list of everyone's contact information." I pointed at Hazel. "She is our unofficial secretary."

"Fine." Marla scribbled her address and birthdate and handed me the pen. "Can I go now?"

Hazel held the door open, and she stalked out.

"Bye." I waved but got nothing except clenched fists and hunched shoulders in response.

"Well, that was unproductive." I slumped onto a chair.

She pointed to the paper. "Oh, no. That went very well. She signed her name under her address and birthdate. And she admitted to sending threatening letters. I think we need to contact Marcus."

AFTER TEXTING Marcus and asking him to call, Hazel and I rounded up the emails and letters and made copies.

"Just in case," Hazel said. She folded the copies and stuck them in the back of her notebook.

My phone rang, and I answered without checking caller ID. "Hey, Marcus, thanks for calling."

"This is Shortie."

My face heated up. "Oh, I'm sorry. I'd texted Marcus to call me."

"Just checking on you and Hazel. Hadn't heard from you in a while."

I punched the speaker button and set my phone on the table. "Marla left. I think we made her mad."

Roscoe added his two cents. "He's the mayor, he's the mayor."

Shortie chuckled. "He's learned new words."

Hazel leaned toward my phone. "He knows plenty of words, but I had to make him unlearn them."

"Sounds like a story. So how did y'all make Marla mad?"

I explained how Marla confessed to sending Sylvia threatening letters. And that we'd gotten her signature.

"She and Sylvia used to be friends. She blamed the affair on Sylvia. She never said anything about her husband's part," I added.

"Well, I am still not finding much about Roger Keaton. Nothing new, anyhow. It's like he and his wife dropped out of sight."

"Maybe someone killed him," Hazel said.

"You keep finding dead bodies." I cringed.

"Actually, that's you."

"She's right, Peg," Shortie said. "Let me know what Marcus says when he calls. I think I'll contact Charlene and see if she knows anything about Keaton."

Shortie hung up, and Hazel helped me clear the table. She plopped into a chair, chin in hand.

I rinsed the dishes and stacked them to dry. "What are you thinking?"

"What if we're missing a suspect?"

I joined her at the table and sighed. My foot ached from all the ups and downs I'd been doing. "What do you mean? Who could we be missing?"

"Roger Keaton's wife."

"Huh?"

Hazel pulled her notebook closer and flipped to the page of our suspects. She tapped the names. "We have Marla and her husband, who was having an affair with Sylvia; Charlene, the anonymous caller; and Roger Keaton. We never considered his wife. What if she's involved?" She sat back and folded her arms.

"He's Charlene's father, but that affair occurred years ago. Why would she do something now?"

"No idea, but she is the only other person we know is connected to Sylvia in all this."

"I'll call Shortie," I said. "He can check into that and find more information on her." My phone rang. "It's Marcus." I hit the accept call and speaker buttons.

"I only have a minute. What did you need?"

"We talked to Marla. Did you know she and Sylvia used to be friends? We have some letters Marla wrote to Sylvia, and in them, she threatened to kill her. We also have emails between Sylvia and the mayor. They're pretty graphic."

"Back up. You have letters threatening Sylvia?"

"Yes."

Marcus huffed out a breath. "How long have you had them?"

"Two days?" Hazel nodded. "Yep, two days. Since Sunday."

He didn't say anything. I jiggled my phone to make sure we hadn't lost our connection. "Marcus? Are you there?"

"Yes."

Uh-oh. "Did you hear what I said?"

"Yes."

Hazel grimaced and bared her teeth. *He's mad,* she mouthed.

No kidding, I thought, clamping my mouth shut. Anything I said now would make matters worse.

Seconds ticked by.

"I'm going to come by, and you're going to give me the letters and emails," he ground out.

"Oh."

"And Peg?"

"Yes?"

"You have to let the police do their job. Please."

"Mm-hmm."

"And just so you know, you've been cleared as a suspect." He hung up, and my phone rang again before I could process his words.

"Marcus, I'll give you the letters and emails."

"Um, Shortie here."

I slapped myself on the forehead and groaned. "Hi."

"I can tell you're glad I called." He chuckled.

"Well, I just got off the phone from a frustrating conversation with Marcus." I put him on speaker and filled him in on what the detective said, ending with, "He was mad."

"I'm sure he is. I shouldn't even help you. The police need to do this job."

I gritted my teeth. "Yes, Marcus keeps reminding me. But you are investigating with us. Admit it, you can't not be involved."

Shortie sighed, but didn't admit to anything. "I called to tell you I contacted Charlene. Her father is in Guatemala. But his wife, Estelle, is in town. I'll try to talk to her."

"That reminds me. Hazel thinks the wife might be a suspect."

"How?"

"If you put Sylvia at the center of all this—kind of like a spider web—the people around her are Marla and Neil Braden, her daughter, and Roger Keaton and his wife," Hazel explained.

"What about the anonymous caller?" Shortie asked.

"I think it's one of these people," she said.

"What motive would Keaton's wife have?"

"Same one as Marla. Discarded wife." I wouldn't just sit back if someone did what Sylvia had. Probably wouldn't murder anyone, but still.

"Okay. You might have a point. I'll try to meet with Estelle and let you know what I find out."

We hung up, and I turned to Hazel. "I have to get out of the house. This is making me crazy."

"Let's go for a drive." She grabbed her wallet and keys while I locked the front door.

"We can run through the sandwich shop drive-through on the way home." My stomach rumbled.

CB barked and trotted after us. All the mystery was getting to me, and I needed to be outside, get some fresh air and sunshine. Hazel drove, CB in the back seat, and I leaned my head on the headrest. She puttered out of the subdivision and down to Nine Mile Road, heading east toward Milton. We crossed the bridge and got off at the first exit in Pace. She pulled up to a small café and parked.

"Let's eat here for something different than our usual sandwich shop. I've heard it's good." She rolled down the windows halfway. A light breeze filled the car, and CB curled up on the backseat. "Sleep well and let us know about any bad guys."

He gave a soft woof.

"Surely, the bad guys stayed in Pensacola." I held the café door for her. Delicious scents enveloped us as we approached the counter. I studied the menu above the cashier's head. "What do you recommend?" I asked.

"Our chicken salad is a favorite," she said.

"Sounds wonderful." Hazel agreed, and we ordered sandwiches with chips on the side.

We grabbed a table beside the window. While waiting for our food, a black two-door sedan drove in and parked beside Hazel's Bug. CB started barking, and I realized the person from the sedan was out of his car and reaching through the window, attempting to open the door to Hazel's car.

"Hazel! Someone is breaking into your vehicle." I pointed, and she rushed outside while I hobbled along behind.

"Hey, that's my car!" Hazel hurried to the stranger.

The sedan's driver, dressed in black with a hoodie pulled over his head, hopped back in the car and revved the engine. He backed up so fast he almost hit Hazel, then stomped the pedal, burning rubber as he roared out of the parking lot.

I grabbed Hazel's arm to steady her while CB continued barking. He jumped out when she opened the car door and stood in the parking lot woofing until she shushed him.

Drawing deep breaths, I rubbed his head. "Smart boy." I frowned. "What happened?"

"I'm not sure, but here." She leaned down and picked up a card from the ground.

"Is that a business card?"

She turned it over and handed it to me. "Yes, and it's for Roger Keaton."

"But Shortie said Keaton is in Guatemala."

She cocked an eyebrow. "According to his daughter."

The mystery of Sylvia's death surrounded me even at a tiny café in a different town. "Let's take our sandwiches to go. We don't want to be here if that person returns."

Chapter 15

I examined Keaton's business card while Hazel drove us home. Nothing was handwritten on it. My hands shook as I tucked it in my purse.

"Did you see the person drop it?"

Hazel kept a firm grip on the steering wheel. "No. Wouldn't we have noticed it when we parked though? If it was already there?" She glanced back at CB. "I'm so glad he's not hurt."

"Me too." I reached back and stroked his soft head. He nuzzled my hand. "Can he have a chip as a reward?"

He barked.

"He understands the word 'reward.' Sure, he can have a couple."

I pulled the chips from the food bag, got one, and pretended to eat it. CB put a paw on my shoulder.

"Here, silly boy." I chuckled and handed it to him. "You're a sweet fellow."

He inhaled it, licked his chops, and turned to me with soulful eyes.

"One more? He won't throw up, will he?" I asked.

"One more should be all right. I'll take a few too." She stuck out her hand.

CB settled on the back seat with the second chip. I offered Hazel the bag, and she grabbed a couple.

"I'm hungry." She banged one hand on the steering wheel. "I hate how that person interrupted our lunch. It's up to us to solve this, Peg."

I unwrapped my sandwich. "I agree." I took a bite, chewed, and swallowed. "This is yummy. Do you want yours now?"

She pulled into my subdivision. "No, we're almost home. I'm going to drive around the long way to check for the black sedan. Whoever it was must have followed us to Pace."

I slumped in my seat. "Probably need to tell Marcus, too."

"Yep, and Shortie."

We sighed in unison.

The coast was clear. Hazel parked the VW in my garage, closing the door behind us. I double-checked the locks on the doors and windows inside the house. It was time to invest in a security system. I wrote myself a sticky note before I forgot.

After finishing lunch, Hazel pursed her lips and crossed her arms. "Guess it's time to call the guys."

"Yeah. Do we have to do it right now?"

"This afternoon was supposed to be a break. How about we watch a little TV?" She settled into her favorite corner of the couch.

"Good idea." I grabbed the remote and my laptop and curled up on the lounge chair. We spent an hour watching fixer-upper programs while I tinkered with the Mamma Birds blog before I turned off the TV. "It's time. If I keep watching this stuff," I gestured to the television, "I'll be at the hardware store, buying paint and flooring."

"That's how I feel. Speaking of houses, I need to check with my insurance company and see when they'll do my roof." She stood and grabbed her phone. "Mind if I call now? Before they close for the day?"

"Go ahead. I'll call the guys. All they're going to do is fuss. You don't have to be here for that."

I waited for her to go to her room before calling Marcus. He didn't answer, so I left a message, and then tried Shortie, who answered on the first ring.

"Hey, what's up? I'm still tracking down Estelle."

Explaining the black sedan and the person trying to break into Hazel's car, plus Keaton's business card, was the easy part of the conversation. Shortie spluttered and fumed —a pattern in my relationships with him and Marcus. Making them mad wasn't what I wanted to do, but I excelled at it.

Someone pounded at the front door, interrupting Shortie's spiel.

"Who is that? You need to check but don't open it. I'll be right over." His staccato instructions made sense, even while they infuriated me.

I stomped to the door. "You and Marcus must think I'm pure stupid." I jerked the door open and found myself nose-to-nose with Marcus. Handing him the phone, I clomped to the couch, sat, and crossed my arms.

He stood in the doorway, holding my phone. "Who is this?"

I gritted my teeth. "Shortie. Talk to him. Y'all can get all your macho testosterone-laden anger out together."

He put it to his ear. Shortie's raised voice reached me across the room, and Marcus's tone wasn't any lower. My annoyance kept me from getting into their conversation. But I heard every word.

Hazel peeked out of her room and cocked an eyebrow. "Is it safe out here?"

"Yep. Fine."

"I'm going back to my room then." She tiptoed back, and her door clicked shut.

I wanted to hide too. Marcus faced the front porch, so I got up and attempted to sneak off. Things were going well until I stepped off the living room carpet onto the kitchen tile, and my boot clomped. Every. Other. Step.

Marcus cleared his throat. I turned, and he was watching me, arms crossed, muscles tight, eyebrows raised, dimple pronounced.

"Something in my room." I stuttered over my words. "Something I need. In my room. Right there." I pointed down the hall. "Be right back." I finished step-clomping till I hit the carpet in my bedroom and shut the door. I leaned against it, drew a deep breath, and blew it out hard. My shoulders slumped. I was not right in the mind. I had this constant push-pull feeling when I was with Marcus. Solving Sylvia's murder should have been my main focus, but his handsome face kept interrupting my thoughts.

A knock on my bedroom door startled me, and I turned too fast, twisting my boot and other foot, landing in a heap.

"Come in." I kept my head down and raised my hand as the door opened. "Help me up, please."

Strong arms reached around and hoisted me to my feet. I held on and looked up straight into Marcus's eyes. "Hi."

His dimple flashed.

"You're laughing at me?"

"Oh, Peg." He chuckled, ducking his head. "I've tried to keep you out of this mess." He released me and bent over, hands on his knees. "I ... I just ..." He laughed until he stood and wiped his eyes. "Boy, I needed that."

My mouth dropped open, but nothing came out. It was hard to reconcile this Marcus with the grumpy detective I knew.

"I know you think I'm a mean guy." He reached out, ran his thumb down my cheek, and stepped closer. "I'm not. I only want you to be safe."

"But you thought I killed Sylvia," I whispered.

"I had to clear you. It's protocol." His thumb brushed my lips.

I leaned in, and he wrapped an arm around me. As his head dipped, a knock sounded at my door, followed by a swish as it opened. A bark preceded Hazel's words, "Shortie's at the front door."

I closed my eyes and dropped my head. Of course he was.

Stepping back, I caught Marcus's expression. He grimaced. "I'll be back." He turned as he left my room. "That's a promise, not a Schwarzenegger impression."

I chuckled, still trying to merge my impressions of him into one man. Most of the times I'd talked to him—starting with Anna's death and investigation—he had been unyielding, obstinate, uncompromising. He was caring, I knew, since he'd visited me at the hospital. According to his story of his wife and daughter, he had suffered a great loss. I'd never heard him laugh before, and the memory made me smile. The thought of the almost kiss sent shivers down my spine.

"Get yourself under control, girl." I checked myself in the mirror over my dresser and headed to the dining room, ignoring Shortie's raised eyebrow.

I pulled out a chair at the table, gesturing for the two men to join me. "Hazel? Come on out here."

She peeked her head out of her room. "Is the coast clear?"

"No," Shortie, Marcus, and I said together.

She joined us, scootching her chair close to mine. Leaning over, she whispered, "What's going on?"

I waved to the two men.

"First off ...," Marcus began.

"I don't understand how these things ...," Shortie said.

He sat back and gestured to Marcus. "Go ahead."

Marcus sighed. "First off, this is a police investigation." He glared at Shortie. "You know that. Why are you involved again?"

Shortie shrugged and lifted his hands. I waited for him to point to me, but he didn't.

Marcus's frustration came through loud and clear. "Here's what I know. You went to eat lunch, and someone tried to break into your car."

"Yes." Hazel inhaled. "We ..."

He held out his hand. "Can I see the business card?"

She retrieved it from the kitchen counter and handed it to him. He examined both sides and tossed it on the table.

"This tells us nothing. We don't know if the person dropped it or not. What can you tell me about the car or the driver?"

Hazel raised her hand. "The vehicle was black."

"Two-door sedan," I added.

"And the thief was dressed all in black."

"Thief?" Shortie chuckled.

Hazel shot him an injured expression. "What else would you call him? You weren't there. He tried to break into my Bug, and CB could've gotten hurt."

CB barked, and Shortie raised his hands. Hazel had never been mad at him. I snorted with laughter and clamped my hand over my mouth.

Marcus's lips twitched. "Back to the thief. What was he wearing? Was it a man?"

"The person was slim, but I do think it was a man," I said. "Dressed in black, and his hoodie was up."

Hazel tapped her chin. "I remember one thing—the license plate was different. Not the traditional Florida one. A specialty plate of some kind, but Florida for sure. I don't remember anything else. Only it was different."

"That helps, Hazel. Thanks." He smiled, and my mother-in-law relaxed a bit.

Shortie cleared his throat. "Can I speak now?"

"Sure." Marcus sat back and crossed his arms.

"I've been checking out several people, but especially Keaton." He turned to Marcus. "I know you don't like me investigating. It's what I do, man. Can't help it. Anyhow, Keaton is in Central America. Guatemala, to be exact. And his wife is in town."

"Estelle," Marcus confirmed.

"Yep. I checked her out because Peg and Hazel suggested she might have a motive to kill Sylvia. Discarded wife and all. Because Keaton was Sylvia's lover years ago, and he's Charlene's father."

"Find anything?" Marcus shifted in his seat.

"Yes, I did." Shortie paused. "Estelle has a driver. He has a black, two-door sedan."

THERE WASN'T much to say after Shortie's announcement. Marcus left to check out the driver and car. Shortie glared at me for a moment before he left. I didn't know what to do or say. Per usual, I shook it off. What else could I do?

The two men hadn't been gone more than a couple of minutes when someone knocked on my door.

I pushed myself off the couch, groaning and muttering.

"What's that?" Hazel said. She was in the kitchen fixing an afternoon cup of decaf for the both of us.

"I'm tired of people knocking on my door." I peered

through the peephole, pulled the door open, and gestured for the visitor to enter.

"I feel so welcome." Lauree threw her arms around me.

"Sorry, it's been a long day." I hugged her and held on tight.

She leaned back and glanced at Hazel. "What's going on? Is she all right?"

Hazel nodded and lifted the coffee pot. "Want some? It's decaf."

"Yes, please." She followed me to the kitchen island, and we perched on the bar stools. "What's up with you two?"

I gripped the mug Hazel handed me, relishing the warmth, and sniffed the brew. Even though it was decaf—often maligned—it would hit the spot. Something to lift me.

Lauree elbowed me.

"Hey, don't make me spill this." I held my cup high.

"You know the expression, 'spill the tea?' Do that, and don't leave out details."

So, I spilled. And Hazel spilled. There was a lot of spillage, and Lauree couldn't close her mouth through the whole thing.

"It's only been two days since I came over," she said when we finished. Her eyebrows were knitted, and she chewed on her lip.

I saluted her with my mug. "Welcome to my world."

"You don't think the mayor had anything to do with Sylvia's death?"

"No, we don't," Hazel said. "He was in a win-win situation. At least, he thought so. Why kill Sylvia?"

"And his wife? Marla?" Lauree held her mug out to Hazel, who refilled it.

"We have those cards from Marla, where she threatens Sylvia, but I just don't see it," I said.

Lauree narrowed her eyes. "What?"

"Oh yeah, I forgot that part." I filled her in on the cards and

144

emails and ended with, "Marcus was supposed to get them when he was here. Guess he forgot."

"Sidetracked by you, I think," Hazel murmured over her coffee mug.

"Hmm, another story?" Lauree walked her fingers up my arm. "What's up with him, Peg?"

I brushed her hand away.

"Don't forget Shortie," my mother-in-law piped up.

"Two men?" Lauree swatted me. "Out of the frying pan and into the fire." She set her chin in her palm, fluttering her eyelashes. "Tell all."

Chapter 16

There wasn't much to tell. Yes, I had two attractive, smart, interesting men in my life. That was it—no big thing.

Lauree's eyebrow twitched up. "Yep, that's it. That's where it ends, right?"

"Not if I can help it." Hazel held her mug up and clinked it with Lauree's.

"Y'all are funny." Not. "I have an idea. Let's check out Florida license plates and see if you can figure out which one was on the sedan."

Hazel got her laptop and settled at the dining table. Lauree and I pulled our chairs close on each side of her. Hazel tapped keys until she got to the Florida Department of Highway Safety and Motor Vehicles website and searched for specialty plates. After saying "Hmmm," and "Ahhh" a few dozen times, she clicked a link. "Dozens and dozens of tags."

I squinted at the screen. "Scroll down."

"They have every variety of special interests, colleges, animals, organizations, even military ones." She stared at the ceiling, lips pursed, eyebrows scrunched.

I touched her arm. "What are you thinking?"

"About the plate I saw." She tapped back through the samples, mumbling about possibilities. "I think it was an orange background. Not EMS, that's orange wording. Hmm ... oh wait." She perked up, eyes sparkling. "I think I found it."

Lauree and I leaned closer. On page nineteen was a tag with an orange background. It showed a female silhouette holding a machine gun. At the bottom were the words—Woman Veteran.

"Huh." I thought back through everything we'd learned. "Woman Veteran," I repeated. "Sylvia, Marla, Estelle. Were they all veterans?"

Hazel opened another tab on her computer. "Maybe so. How old do you think they all were? We can guesstimate when they served."

Marla had said she and Sylvia had been friends, and we guessed they were both in their early sixties. Estelle, Roger Keaton's wife, was more of a question. I called Charlene. She sounded confused by my query, but she said her stepmother was her father's age, sixty-two.

I hung up. "They are, or were, in their early sixties. When would they have served?"

Hazel did the math and decided they could have joined the service in the late '70s, early '80s. In the quiet, Roscoe flitted in his cage and called, "Pretty bird, pretty bird."

I grabbed Hazel's notebook and pen and turned to a clean page. "Let's brainstorm. Think of things the three women had in common." I wrote their names at the top of the page.

"Charlene," Hazel said.

"Birding?" Lauree asked. "Was Estelle into that?"

I added "birding?" to the list.

"Military?" I added it and tapped the pen on my chin.

"Cynthia joined the Navy right after she graduated. What if they did that? Or some branch of service."

Hazel pulled her laptop closer. "We could find out if they attended the same high school." She pointed to me. "Put it on your list."

"Shortie was an MP in Pensacola, right?" Lauree asked.

"Yep. He retired here," I said. "Why?"

"Well, I was thinking of the base, the three women, the birding, and Pensacola. Making some assumptions. Call Charlene and ask where her mom went to high school. And then ask Marla."

"Hazel, will you check with Marla?" I picked up my phone and hit redial. When Charlene answered, I explained parts of what we were attempting to figure out. She said her mother had attended Woodham High School.

"But it's not there anymore. The building is, but it's now Woodham Middle School." She paused. "Why do you want to know?"

"We're trying to make connections between people. Thanks for your help." I hung up. "Whew. She wants answers, and I don't want to explain our thoughts. Yet."

Hazel had gone out front to call Marla, and she rejoined us at the table. "She is suspicious." Hazel grimaced.

"Charlene too."

"But she told me she went to Woodham High."

"Ta-da! Connections! Write that down, Peg." Lauree tapped the page.

I saluted her, scribbled the school's name, and asked, "How do we find out about Estelle?"

Hazel wiggled her eyebrows. "Call Shortie."

Lauree propped her chin on her hand. "Yes, call him." She walked her fingers up my arm again.

"Ugh, you two. You're giving me the shivers."

"No, that's from Shortie." She giggled.

"Or Marcus." Hazel elbowed Lauree.

I sighed. "All right, you two incorrigible women." I tapped Shortie's number on my phone and hit the speaker button. "See, no secrets here."

"Hi, Peg." His husky voice sent more shivers up my spine.

"Hi."

"Hi, Shortie." My mother-in-law winked.

Lauree leaned closer to my phone. "Hey."

"Who's that voice?" he asked.

"That's Lauree. You met her at the first meeting."

"Yep. I remember. So what's up? You three must have something going on."

Lauree covered her mouth, and Hazel put her head on the table, her shoulders shaking with laughter.

"I, or we, were wondering if you could find out where Estelle went to high school?"

"Probably? Why?"

"We found out Marla and Sylvia both attended Woodham. And they're roughly the same age," I said.

Hazel lifted her head. "I think the plate on the sedan was a women's veteran one. What if they were all in the military together?"

"That's a stretch," he said. "But possible. Let me find out more about Estelle."

We all said goodbye, and Hazel returned to tapping on her keyboard.

"Didn't Cynthia use the Delayed Entry Program?" she asked.

"Yes, she did. She signed up midway through her senior year. Did they have that in the '70s?"

She pointed to the screen. "Yes, I think so." She clicked a few keys and read aloud, "'The DEP grants you the opportunity to postpone recruit training for one year to complete high school, graduate from college, or get your affairs in order before starting this life-changing journey.'"

Lauree leaned back in her chair. "We're assuming a lot. How do we know we're right?"

My phone rang. I answered and hit the speaker button. "Hey, Shortie. Did you find out anything?"

"Woodham High, like the other two. Y'all may be onto something."

I explained what we were thinking about the delayed entry program.

"If they did DEP, they were enlisted, not officers," he said.

Hazel raised a finger. She peered closer at her laptop. "Plus, even though The Women's Armed Services Integration Act was enacted in 1948, it wasn't until '78 women were allowed on Navy ships."

"Other than on hospital ships, I think that's true," he said. "But I'm sure women served in onshore positions."

"How do we find out if they did the DEP?" Lauree asked.

I made a face. "Guess we need to call everyone again."

Lauree headed home to check on the twins' homework and start dinner. I texted Charlene, and Hazel texted Marla. Shortie said he had some things to do before he could check into Estelle again. While we waited for return texts, Hazel fed Roscoe and let CB out to run for a bit.

After flipping my wireless speaker on and setting it to the contemporary Christian station, I got out my pressure cooker, stuck frozen chicken thighs in it, and added some water and barbeque sauce. I rummaged in my fridge and found a fresh package of coleslaw, which I stirred into a quick slaw dressing. French fries would round out the meal, but they wouldn't need to be started for another half hour.

I plopped on the couch and propped my boot on the coffee

table. My phone sounded with a text, but it was on the kitchen counter. It could wait. My brain was tired and needed a break.

Hazel returned and joined me, CB curled up between us. He wasn't allowed on my furniture, but we both needed his comfort and warmth today.

She sighed. "What a day."

"Yeah." I leaned my head back and relaxed. "It's hard to believe it was this morning Marla came over."

She crossed her feet on the coffee table. "Mm-hmm. Let's not think about her or any of the others for a bit. Sound good?"

"Sounds perfect."

Next thing I knew, my pressure cooker was chiming it was finished with the barbeque chicken. Then my cell rang. And someone pounded on the door.

Hazel stirred. "I think we both fell asleep."

I rubbed my eyes. "Yep. It was a nice nap."

Chiming, phone ringing, and door knocking continued.

"I don't want to get up."

Hazel stood, stretched side to side, and turned to me. "I'll answer the door. You get the food and your cell."

I placed a towel over the steam outlet on the pot and slid the button to vent. My phone rang again.

"Oh, it's Chloe." I answered as Lauree bustled into my kitchen.

"Chloe's trying to reach you." Lauree's face was drawn and pale.

At the same time, my daughter said, "Mom, Mom, something's wrong." She was crying, and Tom was speaking in the background.

He got on the line. "Peg, she is having some bleeding. I'm taking her to Gulf Breeze Hospital."

Sirens sounded. "Are you there now?" My stomach flipped, and panic flooded my body.

"Yes." His voice was strained. "Parking and going in the ER."

"I'll be right there." I hung up and turned. "I need to go to her."

Lauree wrung her hands. "She called me when you didn't answer. I didn't want to overwhelm her with questions. What's going on?"

My body trembled. "Tom said she was bleeding. They're at the hospital. What if she loses the baby? She just found out she was pregnant." A sob escaped my lips.

"I can take you if you need. You can't drive right now."

Hazel hurried into the room. "I have our purses, Peg. Lauree, can you feed CB and let him out to potty? He'll be fine here until we're home. Roscoe is fine for the night. I'll drive Peg to the hospital." She set a can of dog chow on the counter. "Do you have a house key?"

Lauree nodded.

"Let's go." Hazel tugged my arm and rushed me into the garage.

I sat in the passenger seat, my mouth dry and my mind blank. I closed my eyes and tried to concentrate, but my thoughts bounced all over, and I couldn't capture any of them. "I can't pray, will you?"

"On it." She backed out and roared up the street, hooking a right out of the neighborhood. "Dear Lord,"—she honked at a driver taking too long at a green light—"please hold our Chloe in your hands. Keep the sweet baby safe." She maneuvered around the car in front of us and pulled to the far right to merge onto I-10. "I pray for wisdom for the doctors and nurses. And peace, dear Lord." She took the turn for Interstate 110 and floored it.

"And protection for us," I added with a shaky smile.

"My car doesn't get to high speeds."

I cocked an eyebrow as we whizzed past everyone else, grabbed the edge of my seat with one hand and the armrest with the other, mentally hurrying her. "You're doing great."

Gulf Breeze Hospital was only a couple miles after the bridge between Pensacola and Gulf Breeze. Hazel skidded through a yellow light and turned left into the parking lot. She parked, and we clutched our purses and hoofed it toward the emergency room.

Tom and Chloe weren't anywhere in the waiting room. Approaching the desk, I drew several deep breaths to slow my racing heart.

"Can I help you?" the receptionist asked. Her cheerful smile and animal-covered scrubs were in direct contrast to my mood.

"My son-in-law brought my daughter in. She's pregnant and bleeding."

"Yes, ma'am." She hopped up and pointed to a set of double doors. "Ask the nurse, and she'll show you what room to go to."

"Thanks." I rapped the desk with my knuckles. Hazel followed me.

We pushed through the doors, and the nurse stood as we approached.

"My daughter, Chloe Blackburn, is here." My teeth chattered as I spoke. I couldn't hold my body still.

"Yes, she's over there." She gestured to the left of her desk.

"Here we are, Peg." Tom leaned out of a room and waved.

I rushed to my daughter and wrapped her in my arms, leaned back, and thumbed tears from her cheeks. "Have you seen anyone yet?"

Chloe shook her head.

"They brought us right back," Tom said. "And a tech drew blood."

She wrapped her arms around her belly. "What if I lose the baby?" She moaned.

My son-in-law pulled up a chair on the other side of her bed, and Hazel patted her leg. I rubbed her shoulder, sniffling back tears. It wouldn't help her if I cried.

"Let's see what they say," Hazel said.

She was right. We needed to wait. I tried again to pray.

Finally, the doctor came in. He ordered an ultrasound, and we all cried when the baby's clippity-clop heartbeat filled the room. There wasn't much to see on the screen, but he assured us Chloe and the baby were fine.

"Sometimes a little bleeding happens early in a pregnancy," he explained as he wiped the jelly off her stomach. "You did the best thing coming to get checked out. Go home and stay off your feet. Contact your obstetrician in the morning. They may want you to go on bed rest for a few weeks. You'll have to see what they recommend."

Tom huffed out a breath, his shoulders dropping. "Thank you."

The doctor patted Chloe's foot and left the room.

"Bed rest?" Her voice wobbled.

"Honey, you'll figure it out." I rubbed her arm. "We'll do whatever we can to help." I drew a deep breath and exhaled slowly. The good news was sinking in.

"Focus on that sweet baby," Hazel added.

Chloe smiled and touched her stomach. "Can you believe that heartbeat?"

We all laughed and chatted until the nurse came in with her discharge papers.

Tom pushed Chloe's wheelchair to the parking lot, and Hazel turned to me, eyebrows drawn together. "What if I go stay with her? Until she talks to her doctor?"

"Yes. I think that's a good idea. Makes me feel better to have you there."

Hazel hurried ahead and spoke to Tom and Chloe. I joined them at the car.

"Grandma's going to stay and help me." Chloe's face was drawn and tired, her smile shaky.

"I like that idea." I hugged her and kissed her forehead.

"I'll ride with them." Hazel passed me her keys. "You can come for me once we know what her doctor advises. Text me when you get home."

I hugged them all goodbye with another extra-long squeeze for my daughter. "I love you," I whispered in her ear.

The day began with coffee with Marla this morning and ended at the hospital with Chloe. So much had happened. And so many emotions to process. I drove on autopilot over the three-mile bridge back into Pensacola and found my house pitch black. In our rush to leave, we hadn't thought to leave any lights on inside or out. I pulled into the garage and sat for a moment, taking deep breaths and allowing the stress to leave my body, the baby's heartbeat replaying in my mind. I entered the house through the door into the laundry room, turned on that light, stepped into the kitchen, and reached for the light switch. Something was different. A presence, a scent. Something sweaty and foul. And CB wasn't barking.

I flipped the switch.

Chapter 17

I tried to look everywhere at once, but it was impossible. Someone had strewn my utensils on the kitchen floor, left drawers and cabinets wide open, and overturned the pressure cooker. Barbeque chicken dripped off the counter and plopped on the floor. I edged farther toward the living room and peeked around the wall.

My stomach sank. The couch cushions had been ripped, and the insides shredded, scattered throughout the room. The buffet doors were open—photo albums, placemats, and all the extras I'd shoved in there were now on the carpet.

"Roscoe?" I hurried to the birdcage, stepping around the worst of the damage, and peered inside his cage. He stared back. "What happened here?" I made kissy noises at him.

He crouched in the corner, feathers tucked close to his body, and he didn't make a peep.

"Hey, buddy, you okay?" I opened the latch and reached in. He shuffled farther away from me.

I shut the door. "Poor guy, you're scared." I stood and surveyed the room. "CB? Where are you, fellow?" I clapped. "Come on, talk to me. Where are you?"

No bark answered. No sound at all.

Should I explore the rest of the house? Nothing like this had ever happened before. Someone had trashed my house—at least the kitchen and living room. My dining table was intact. I stared at the front door.

It was unlocked. I knew we'd locked it when we left for the hospital, and I hurried to turn the lock before retracing my steps to the kitchen. My bedroom door was pulled shut, and from where I stood, I saw the front and middle bedroom doors were closed. During the day, we always left them open. Even the hall bathroom door was shut. I couldn't see Hazel's room from where I stood.

Contemplating calling the police and searching the rooms for CB battled in my mind. I couldn't leave Charlie Brown behind. What if he was injured? What if the intruder took him? The thought spurred me on, and I opened my bedroom door with a swish. It was empty. No intruder, no destruction, and after peeking into the master bathroom and closet, I knew CB wasn't there either.

I grabbed the toilet bowl brush, with a nervous laugh, and held it in front of me while I checked the front bedroom and its closet—nothing. Next was the middle room where Hazel had stored the animals' supplies—all fine in there, but no dog. The hall bath was an easy inspection. Nowhere to hide a Weimaraner except the tub, and it was empty. Hazel's bedroom, door closed, was the final place he might be. I shifted the toilet brush to my left hand and turned the doorknob with my right. CB had to be in here. I inhaled and thrust open the door.

Sweet CB lay on Hazel's bed. I stepped closer and poked him. He didn't move. "Hey, buddy." I leaned closer and saw his tummy rise with each breath. I dropped the brush on the carpet, sank onto the bed beside him, and ran my hands over his body. "Charlie Brown? CB?" I patted his head and lifted it onto my lap. Tears streamed down my cheeks, leaving wet splotches on his gray fur.

"You gotta be all right. What am I going to tell your mama?" Thinking about telling Hazel that CB was sedated or hurt was a punch in the gut. She loved the dog. I loved the dog.

I jiggled and poked him again. He stirred and let out a whimper, one eye opening a bit. "Oh, Charlie Brown, you're going to be fine." I swiped my face and pulled my phone out of my back pocket. "I'm going to call Marcus so he can help us."

CB and I waited in Hazel's room for the police. It was almost two in the morning, and I'd requested they not come with sirens blaring. I may not be getting any sleep, but no need to frighten the neighborhood.

CB whimpered again and cuddled closer to me when someone banged on the front door. I picked his head up, stood, and set it down. "It's only Marcus, boy. I'll be back. Help is here." CB's tail swished once.

More banging. I hurried to unlock the door. Marcus rushed in and took me in his arms. He stepped back and surveyed my body and face.

"Are you all right? Are you hurt?" He hugged me again.

"I'm fine." I grunted. "You're squeezing me."

"I'm sorry." He let go but stared at me. "You're fine? I came as quick as I could." He scrutinized the living room. "What's going on? Is someone here?" He noticed the kitchen. "That's a mess."

"I know. I'm fine. CB seems to be sedated or something. No one else is here, I already checked."

Another squad car pulled up, and he stepped outside to talk to his fellow officers. A plop sounded from Hazel's room, and I turned to find CB wobbling toward me.

I kneeled. "Hey, buddy." He sniffed my fingers and sat, still shaky. I helped him lie down. "Stay right there." I couldn't stop running my hands over his body, so thankful he wasn't hurt badly. Petting him comforted me too.

Marcus returned, followed by two men in uniform.

He pointed to one. "You, go investigate that side. There are closets in the garage too." He waved the other officer to the left side of the house. "Three bedrooms and a bathroom on this side. Double check the closets."

They hurried off.

"I told you I searched everywhere. They're just doing what I did."

"We need to make a thorough check." Marcus knelt beside me and patted the dog. "Well look at this guy." He scratched behind CB's ears. "You're a smart fellow. How are you feeling?"

CB licked his fingers. Marcus gave him another scratch and pushed up to stand.

"I'd call his vet. He'll need to be checked over." He put his hands on his hips. "It's the middle of the night. What happened here?"

I explained about Chloe, that we hadn't left lights on, and how I came home to the mess.

"You didn't see anyone or hear anything?"

"No. At first, I smelled something weird." I gestured to the kitchen. "The spilled barbeque, I'm sure."

He winced. "Next time, leave the house and call nine-one-one," he said in a grave voice.

"I had to find CB."

He closed his eyes and groaned. "Peg, please. We'll need to dust for prints, and I'll help you clean this up." He tugged me up off the floor and clicked his tongue at CB. "Let's have you two wait out front."

I settled into the rocking chair, Charlie Brown snuggled on top of my feet. He perked up, and his ears twitched at the police officers in the yard. I dozed until Marcus touched my shoulder.

"It's only me." He smoothed my hair.

It was still dark out. "What time is it?"

He checked his watch. "Almost four. Sunrise is a couple hours away." He gestured to the front door. "Let's get you two inside."

CB stood and trotted into the house. He looked no worse for wear, but I planned to call the vet when their office opened.

Marcus wielded the toilet bowl brush. "My officers found this in Hazel's room. Do you know why it was there?"

I hung my head and scuffed the carpet with my toe. "It was my weapon."

He stepped closer. "Your what?" His lips twitched.

"Weapon. It was in the heat of the moment. I checked my room and bathroom and grabbed it. Just in case."

"In case you what? Had to clean a toilet?"

"Yep. That was my plan. Find CB, find the bad guy, and clean a toilet." I made a silly face.

"Why don't you go lay down and sleep? You're a little punchy." Marcus sat on the couch. "I'll hang out here."

I didn't argue. As I headed toward my room, I noticed the kitchen was spic and span.

"You cleaned up in here?"

He shot me a tired smile. "Yep."

The living room had also been put back together. He patted the couch cushions. "You'll need a new sofa or a seamstress. I stuffed what I could back inside."

I grabbed a sheet and blanket from the hall closet and handed them to him. "Stretch these over the cushions for now. And Marcus"—I touched his shoulder—"thank you for … everything."

～

Mid-morning light filtered through the blinds in my room and woke me. I stretched and checked the clock, then jumped out of bed. Without thinking, I ran into the living room and found Marcus sitting on the couch with a cup of coffee and reading the news on his phone.

"It's ten. Why didn't you wake me?"

He turned and laughed, pointing at my head and making a circle with his finger. "You might want to brush your hair." He smirked.

I clamped both hands on my head, scurried back into my room, and peered in the bathroom mirror.

"This isn't bedhead. This is wind tunnel head," I muttered. After a hot shower, where I used a lot of conditioner, I dressed and rejoined Marcus again in the living room.

"Better?" I curtsied.

"Much."

CB lay beside him on the couch. I sat on the dog's other side. "You're doing better." I stroked his fur, and he wagged his tail. "Guess I need to call the vet."

Marcus scratched CB's head. "Good idea. We dusted for prints last night. So far, nothing has come up. But we'll need a list of people that have been here."

Oh, fun. All the birders, my kids, Lauree. I huffed.

He reached across the back of the couch and tugged a strand of my hair. "Any idea what's going on?"

This was calm Marcus, and I wasn't sure what to say or do. Usually, he was such a take-charge kind of guy.

I tipped my head. "You seem very ... composed."

"You're used to me acting like a bull in a China shop?"

His words, not mine. "Yep."

He leaned forward, propped his elbows on his thighs, and

162

swiped his hands over his face. "Last night was a wake-up call, Peg. For me. And for you."

"What do you mean?"

"Well, it's obvious you've made someone mad or scared. You're in danger." He chewed on his bottom lip.

"What about you? How was it a wake-up call for you?"

He stood and held out his hand. I took it, and he pulled me up close to him. He bent his head. I closed my eyes.

And the doorbell rang.

He leaned his forehead against mine. "I'm going to tear that thing out."

I grimaced. Saved by the bell? My emotions were all over the place, and now was not the time to start anything with Marcus. I still hadn't decided if I wanted a relationship. There hadn't been any time to think about him or Shortie.

My cell chimed as I headed toward the front door. Marcus handed it to me.

"I'll get the door. I think this is your daughter."

Chloe. My stomach flipped. I hadn't thought to check on her this morning. Or tell Hazel what had happened. I answered the phone. Behind me, Marcus opened the door.

"Mom, it's me." Chloe's voice sounded strong, and relief flowed through my body.

I plugged my other ear to hear her. "How are you, honey? Feeling any better?"

"I think so. I called my doctor. They want me to stay off my feet, and they scheduled a checkup for next week."

"That's good news. I was so scared. I know you and Tom were also." I dropped onto the couch. A breath whooshed out of me as the cushion puffed out air too. I'd have to search for a new sofa. My shoulders drooped thinking about what had happened.

"Do you mind if Grandma Hazel stays here a few more days?"

Her question drew me out of my worries. "Yes, of course. She'll be a big help."

Chloe laughed. "She brought me breakfast in bed. It's nice to be waited on."

"Your grandmother has done a one-eighty here. She always seemed ... needy. But she's stepped up."

"She told me about your investigation." Curiosity laced her words.

My mouth dropped open. Now was not the time to tell Hazel or Chloe about last night. I struggled to keep my tone light. "She did? She's enjoyed it, I think. The intrigue."

She giggled. "I could tell. She practically bounced in her seat telling me."

"Ask her about how she opens a locked door."

"I will. Thanks for the suggestion." Chloe paused. "I like having her here. She makes me think of Dad." Her voice grew thick at her last words.

"I know, honey. Ask her stories about him too. She'll enjoy telling them."

"You got home all right last night?"

My daughter's innocent question set butterflies loose in my stomach. "Yes, everything is fine." No way I would worry either her or Hazel. "Tell Grandma Roscoe and CB are doing well."

We said our goodbyes—Chloe promising to update me daily and call with any concerns. I turned and found Shortie and Marcus staring at me.

Chapter 18

Shortie listened quietly to the details of the night before and Marcus's explanation for why he was at my house so early.

His silence confused me. "You guys want breakfast?"

Marcus raised his hand. "Sure."

Shortie humphed, which I deciphered as a yes.

I mixed up pancake batter and set the table, adding butter, syrup, and extra napkins. The pancakes browned at the edges, and I flipped them until they were cooked through.

"Y'all want eggs?"

Both men said no.

I pulled out three plates and piled food on each. Carbs would help. At least, I hoped so.

CB picked a spot between the two men and waited, his eyes darting from one to the other.

Shortie finished his pancakes and wiped his face with his napkin. He set it down and placed his hands on each side of his plate, his gaze piercing me.

"Why didn't you call me?"

"I ... I called the police." I pointed to Marcus with my fork.

Shortie's head dipped. "Message received." He stood, patted CB, and headed for the front door. "Let me know when the next birding trip is. Fort Pickens would be fun." And he left.

My mouth dropped open. "What's up with him?" I frowned at Marcus. "What did you say to him?"

Marcus cleared his throat. His lips twitched. Another throat clearing, and he spoke. "Let's just say Shortie understands where your interest is, where your loyalties are."

"What? What do you mean?"

He held his hands up like scales, one above the other. He wiggled the higher one. "This is me." A wiggle for the lower hand. "This is Shortie."

"Pfft. You men. Not everything is a competition." What he said irked me. I didn't know what I wanted or didn't want. How could either of them know? It may have been years since Zack died, but maybe I wasn't ready to let go of him. Of our love. Of my memories.

Plus, there was the scale thing. Which man would be higher if *I* judged them?

I collected the dirty dishes and loaded the dishwasher.

"Don't take your irritation out on them." Marcus smirked.

I bit the inside of my cheek and pointed to the front door. "Don't you have a job to do today? Catching some bad guys or something? Since you now know I'm not the killer." Apparently, I was still a little salty about being a suspect. I grabbed the dish liquid and sponge and scrubbed the skillet, forcing myself not to rub the finish off of it.

"Yep." He scooted his chair back and stood. "See y'all later." He threw a salute my way and patted CB. He was out the door before I said anything else.

After I dried my hands and spread the kitchen towel out to dry, I locked the front door and found CB's leash. "Come on, fellow, we need a break."

Roscoe piped up, "Pretty bird, pretty bird."

His bird talk made me smile. "I'm glad you feel better." I added some birdseed to his bowl and blew him a kiss. "Wish you could go with us, but the seagulls would carry you off."

CB CLIMBED into the backseat of my Rav, and I buckled into the driver's seat. I hooked a right out of my neighborhood, a left on Olive Road, and a right on Davis Highway. CB agreed I needed more coffee, so we drove through McDonald's before getting on the interstate. I stuck my cup in the SUV's cupholder and took a sharp turn to enter I-110. From there, it was a straight shot, more or less, into Gulf Breeze and over the Bob Sikes Bridge to the beach.

We both needed sunshine and fresh air. I rolled all the windows down, and CB stuck his head out as we crossed the beach bridge. His ears flapped in the breeze.

My hair blew in my face and stuck to my lip. I brushed it back. "Guess where we're going, buddy?"

His ears perked up.

"The cross. It's my favorite place."

CB woofed.

For decades, the Pensacola Beach cross stood as a landmark for Gulf Breeze and Pensacola residents. It was placed on the Sound side of Fort Pickens Road in the 1950s to commemorate the first mass celebrated in 1559 and then relocated to a Gulf-side sand dune several years later.

It was the first stop I made at the beach. The cross had survived all the hurricanes since it was erected. That amazed me. It gave me hope for myself. To be strong, stable, purposeful.

I parked near the cross and let CB out, clipping on his leash.

"We can't go right up to it." I pointed. "See this fencing? It's to help with erosion. But we can stand near it."

CB waited while I whispered prayers—for my kids, for me, for strength and wisdom. Was I betraying Zack by laying down my memories and feelings? I didn't know what to do.

After, I squatted beside CB and raised my phone. My boot made it awkward, and I had to hold onto him to keep from tipping over.

"Selfie time."

He licked my face when I snapped the picture.

"You nut!" I hugged him and stood. "I'm going to send this to your mom." I added the photo to Hazel's number, and my phone "whooshed" when the text sent.

Tromping in the sand would be impossible while wearing the boot. I found a picnic table and sat facing the Gulf, elbows propped on the table behind me. CB woofed at seagulls and nosed the sand but spent most of his time sprawled out in the late September sunshine. When my stomach growled, we hopped back into the SUV in search of lunch.

We stopped at a walk-up restaurant and ordered fish, fries, and coleslaw. I added soda for me and a cup of water for CB, and we sat at a picnic table to wait for our food. My phone dinged. Hazel had responded to the selfie I'd sent.

> Fun! I love that cross. Will you stop by
> Chloe's before you go home?

> Of course. I'm getting something to eat
> now. We'll be over in an hour or so.

My name was called, and I asked for a foam bowl to pour CB's water into. He helped me eat the French fries while I munched on my fish and coleslaw. With our bellies full, I threw the trash away, and we headed back to the car.

"Want to go see your mom and Chloe?"

CB barked.

"You're going to be an uncle. Or wait,"—I did the genealogical line in my head—"maybe you'll be a great uncle?" I giggled. "I'm not sure."

CB BARKED, wiggled, and squirmed when we pulled into Chloe's driveway. Hazel stood on the front porch, and as soon as he got out, he bounded to her.

I chuckled. "He missed you."

She ran her hands over his body and kissed the top of his head. "I've missed you, too, my boy." After giving him lots of pets, she asked, "How is Roscoe?"

Last night's fear and craziness ran through my mind. I forced a calm expression, determined not to tell her what happened. "He's fine. He let me feed him this morning."

"Good. I'm glad." She held the door for me. "Come on in. Chloe is resting on the couch."

I followed her into the living room and leaned down to hug Chloe. I perched on the coffee table beside her. "How are you? Last night was scary."

"Very." She ran her hand over her still-flat belly. "The bleeding has stopped."

"And you're supposed to stay on bed rest, right?"

"Yes, Mom." Her lips twitched, and she pointed to Hazel. "Grandma is watching me like a hawk."

We all laughed, and the tension in my body fled. Everything would be fine. My daughter and grandbaby were healthy, and the scare at my house was over.

Hazel sat in the recliner and raised the footrest. "Speaking of hawks, when is the next birding outing?"

"I haven't even thought of that. And Shortie is mad at me."

"Why? I thought you two were getting along?"

Uh-oh. "Well, he ..."

"Grandma tells me you have two men interested in you, Mom." Chloe interrupted, eyebrows wiggling. "When were you going to tell me?"

"You two! That's not true." I stood and crossed the room to gaze out the back window, thankful she changed the subject, but not necessarily to this one.

"Shortie and Marcus. Both are nice men and very good-looking." Hazel stressed how handsome they were. "Your mother is in denial."

I turned. "Hazel! Don't fill her head with that."

"Mom, it's fine. Daddy's been gone for years. You're still young enough to meet someone."

"I'm still young enough," Hazel mumbled.

Both of us turned to her. I tapped my chin. "Hmm, now that I think of it, Owen is the perfect age for you."

Chloe clapped. "Who is that?"

I sat at the end of the couch by her feet. "He's handsome and a retired professor." I filled her in on all of Owen's wonderful qualities.

"Sounds nice, Grandma. Maybe that's what you need."

Hazel pointed at us. "You two. Quit." She rubbed her hand down CB's side. "This fellow and Roscoe are my guys. I'm fine." She gestured with her thumb at her chest. "I do not need a man."

"Tell me more about this Owen guy, Mom." Chloe scooted around on the couch, and I helped her get a pillow in a comfortable position.

We teased Hazel until Tom came home.

I stood and kissed his cheek. "I better get going. Not rushing out because you're home, Tom. It's later than I thought." And I knew I didn't want to arrive home in the dark.

I kissed Chloe goodbye, and Hazel walked CB and me to the SUV. I got in and rolled down my window. "I'll check on you guys tomorrow."

Hazel had a thoughtful look on her face. She tipped her head. "Is something going on, Peg? Something you're not telling me?"

I struggled to maintain an innocent air. "We're fine. No new news."

She pursed her lips and stepped back. "Be careful. Bye, CB." She blew him a kiss.

As I drove home, I reassured myself I hadn't lied to my mother-in-law. It was true there was no new news. She didn't need to know about the night before. Not yet.

BUTTERFLIES FLUTTERED in my stomach when I got to my subdivision and went on full attack as I pulled up to my house. I parked in the garage and let CB out of the car. Taking a deep breath, I opened the door to the house and allowed him to go first. He trotted right in without hesitation, and I followed at a slower pace, sniffing the air for suspicious scents. All I smelled was the syrup from breakfast.

Roscoe piped up, "Birds alive, birds alive!"

"New phrase?" I waved to him and set my purse on the island. "Where did you learn that?"

"Birds alive!" he screeched again.

I crossed the room and peered into his cage. "Calm down, Roscoe. Only me and CB here." I glanced around. The front door was locked, and the rest of the house appeared how it had when we left. Relief flowed through me.

Sleeping alone in the house wasn't my idea of fun. I'd grown accustomed to Hazel being there, and Marcus protected me the night before. But exhaustion won. CB slept in my room, and his doggie snoring soothed me.

New ideas and directions for the investigation filled my mind in the morning. I needed Hazel's notebook, but I didn't know where she kept it and didn't want to dig through her things. I texted her, and she called me within minutes.

"You didn't have to call. I wanted your notebook. Do you have it with you?"

"No, I didn't think to take it in our rush. What are you working on?"

How much should I say? "I am going to check back through everything. See if anything new pops out."

"Okay. You're sure you're not keeping something from me?" Curiosity rang in her voice.

I bit my lip and thought about what to say, "We're all fine, promise. Here, Roscoe has a new saying." I turned to the bird. "Hey, buddy. Can you tell your mom what you told me?"

Roscoe stared at me, turned, and faced the wall—moody bird.

I chuckled. "Well, he's not feeling talkative. He's pouting."

"How would he learn a new phrase? Did you teach it to him?"

"No, why?"

"He doesn't make up words, Peg. What did he say?"

Oh my. It hadn't crossed my mind Roscoe had to hear the expression. "Birds alive. And he said it like with an exclamation at the end." I imitated the parakeet's squawk for her.

Roscoe's head popped up. "Birds alive!" His screech startled CB, who responded with a sharp woof.

"Did you hear him?" I asked Hazel.

"Yes. Where did *he* hear that?" Suspicion laced her words.

"I don't know. I really don't." Where did that bird learn those words? Had the intruder said them? It had to be that. I never used the phrase.

"Keep an eye on him. I'm not sure where he picked it up. It's nothing I've heard him say."

"I will. Back to your notebook. Where is it?"

She told me to search in or on her nightstand. When we hung up, I exhaled. Crisis averted. Maybe the intruder said, "Birds alive," and that's how Roscoe learned the expression. I couldn't be sure. Hazel was suspicious though, and I'd have to be careful what I said.

I sat at the dining table with her notes, a pen, and a fresh pad of paper. I started at the beginning and read through what she'd written, jotting ideas on my notepad. Then I went back to the beginning again and tried to connect the dots, rewriting the first list:

1. Birdseed at Sylvia's?
2. Receipt for which kind?
3. Sylvia's killer?
4. Why was she killed?
5. Did the killer know where I lived?

We had solved the first question about the birdseed— Sylvia hadn't grabbed the wrong kind. The killer had planted it. And the killer, or someone working with them, knew where I lived.

I circled number three—Sylvia's killer. That still hadn't been answered—by the police or by me.

Chapter 19

I reviewed our list of suspects. Per Marcus, Marla and Neil Braden were out of the running, leaving Charlene, Roger Keaton, and the anonymous caller. I added Estelle Keaton and wrote another list beside that one with the names Marla, Sylvia, and Estelle. Then I drew an arrow from them to Woodham High School, and underneath wrote DEP.

If all three women had entered the military through the Delayed Entry Program and served together, had there been rivalry? Under DEP, I put rivalry—job and men.

So many questions. I tapped my pen on the paper. I'd thought of something early this morning. One question we hadn't answered. I picked up my cell and called Hazel.

"I'm searching my memory, and it's failing me."

She laughed. "Welcome to my world."

"It's something someone mentioned. I can't remember." I read my notes aloud to her.

"Sylvia? Something she said when you found her?"

"No, she didn't say anything." My mind whirred. "It's like there are file cabinets in my head, and the right one isn't opening. Grrr." I smacked my pen down. "Maybe coffee will help."

"Coffee helps everything. Make some and call me back when you remember."

I brewed a pot—full-strength, dark roast—settled on the couch, and flipped on the TV, wondering if something had happened with Sylvia's investigation. I was mid-sip when the station put up a picture. The heading read 'Salute to Veterans' followed by a former military person's name and branch of service.

I grabbed Hazel's notes from the dining table and reread the part about Marla, Sylvia, and Estelle serving in the military. Hazel was sure the license plate on the black sedan at the café was an orange-colored woman veteran one.

I drank more coffee, wracking my memory, read the list, and tapped my pen on each name, thinking through what we'd learned. We still didn't know who the anonymous caller was, and I had never talked to either Keaton, so my pen stopped on Charlene. "It was her. I know it was her."

I called Hazel again, and she answered before it rang on my end.

"Were you sitting on top of your phone?"

"I knew you'd call back. Did you remember?"

"No."

She sighed.

"But," I said, "it was something Charlene mentioned. Think back to when you, Shortie, and I met with her. She mentioned something, and I forgot to ask her about it. Do you remember that?"

After a long pause on the other end of the line, Hazel squawked, "Got it!"

I jumped. "You have got to quit doing that." I drew a deep

breath, blew it out, and fanned my face. "My heart rate is slowing down now. What did you think of?"

"Birding. She said something about her mom and birding."

"Yep, that's it. Sylvia mentioned at our first meeting how she used to take Charlene birding with her."

"Yes, and Charlene said it stopped when she was older or a teen or something. But then she said something else …" Hazel hummed. "I'm going over that meeting in my mind. It's like a steel trap."

My eyes were getting tired of rolling.

Hazel hummed for another minute. "She said birding had caused all the problems. Something like that."

"Yes!" I smacked the table.

Roscoe piped up, "Birds alive!" And CB barked.

"What, what is it?" Hazel asked.

"I said her mother loved birding. And she said that's what caused all this trouble."

"You're right. And we never questioned her more. How could birding cause trouble and cause Sylvia's death? That's extreme."

"Very extreme. From the little I've learned about the birding world, though, it's competitive. Birders want to be the one to find the rarest bird. I'm sure with some people, it's cutthroat." An image of Sylvia dying in front of me flashed through my mind, and my stomach flipped.

"When is Sylvia's funeral? Can you call Charlene and ask? We can talk to her and investigate who shows up for it."

I scribbled a note to find out. "Sure. I'll let you know. I want to check on Anna too. Find out if there is going to be a service for her. Before we hang up, how are my daughter and my grandbaby?"

Hazel filled me in on Chloe, who had calmed down and was napping. We chatted about where to shop for baby things and hung up. I decided to make a salad for lunch. Afterward, I'd call Charlene.

I stretched lunchtime out as long as possible. Calling Charlene wasn't at the top of my list. Shortie had talked to her a few times—maybe I should call him. Would he speak to me, though? He was upset when he left the day before, and Marcus had compared himself to Shortie. Thinking about that made me angry all over again. As much as I liked his dimples, Marcus had an arrogance and unkindness that turned me off. It reminded me of my dad. He'd had that cocky attitude too and used it on my mom and me to get his way.

Plus, the way Marcus had weighed himself against Shortie. That wasn't fair. For me, Marcus's overconfidence outweighed his attractiveness. It told me something about him I hadn't known before.

I grabbed my cell, and without thinking it through, I called Shortie. My call went straight to voicemail, so I left a short message. I cleaned my lunch dishes, dried my hands, and leaned against the kitchen counter. Movement through the blinds caught my attention. My heart pounded, and I tripped trying to get to the door and peek through the peephole. Marcus stood on the doorstep. I took a deep breath and huffed it out as I opened the door.

"Hi." I bit my lip. No smiling or flirting with him today.

His police car was parked at the curb, and he was in uniform—tall, handsome, and flashing the dimple—leaning against the door jamb. "You okay?"

"Yep. Why are you here?"

He straightened and backed up, hands held in front of him. "Are you mad at me?"

A Jeep pulled into my driveway, and my heart dropped. Shortie was here. Great, another repeat of yesterday. Not on my watch.

I turned back to Marcus. "No, I'm fine. What did you need?"

His expression hardened. His tone all business, he said, "I forgot to get those emails and letters from you the other day."

"Yep, hang on." I closed the door in his face and called Shortie. "Wait in your car. Marcus is about to leave."

"Right." His tone was abrupt, and I couldn't blame him, but I wasn't about to let him be insulted again. He was getting the short end of the stick in all of this.

Whether or not I knew what I wanted—if anything—Shortie was a good guy and my friend.

The stack of emails and letters sat beside the copier. I scooped them up, wrapped a rubber band around them, and opened the front door. "Here."

Marcus took them. "Are *we* all right?"

I sighed and gestured toward Shortie. "I need to talk to him. Can you go?" My mother would spank me for my rudeness, but what else could I do?

He clicked his tongue. "Sure thing." He turned and marched up the steep yard to his cruiser.

After he drove off, I waved Shortie to the house.

He tromped up the front walk and stopped in front of me, hands jammed in his shorts' pockets. "What's up?" His eyes, usually so kind, were flat and emotionless.

"I need to apologize to you. I've been sending mixed messages, and I'm sorry. Marcus, well, he was rude to you too. But I can't speak for him." I opened the door and stepped aside. "Will you come in so we can talk?"

I thought he would nod and come in, but he stepped closer and bent down to me.

His kiss—warm, tender, gentle, and commanding all at the same time—was not what I expected him to do.

Oh my. I touched my lips. A shiver ran through me. No,

more like an electric shock. I followed him into my house and shut the door, leaning against it.

He walked to the couch and sat, patting the cushion beside him. "Peg? Come sit by me."

I sat at the edge of the couch like a statue.

He chuckled. "Guess I caught you off guard."

Get yourself under control. Just because that's the first kiss you've had since Zack died doesn't mean you can't be normal. I cleared my throat. "No, nope, I'm fine."

His lips twitched. I caught myself staring at them and forced myself to look away. I shoved my hands under my legs to avoid touching my mouth again.

Shortie leaned forward and touched my arm, his gaze soft and warm. "I came here to apologize to you."

I frowned. "Why?"

"I got into some kind of competition with Marcus. That's not me." He barked a laugh. "You know that, right? I don't want you to think I'm that kind of guy. We're friends, and I'm happy with that. If you are?"

"Yes, friends. I like that." I turned to him. "It was a nice kiss. A bit more than friends?"

"There's more where that comes from." He sat back, spreading his arm across the back of the couch. "But it's all on your terms. How's that sound?"

I liked that—my terms. Marcus was, as he said, a bull in a China shop. Shortie wasn't like that. Neither man was anything like Zack. I wouldn't want them to be. I had figured that much out.

"Got it. Sounds good to me."

"So, why did you call?"

I shifted to the other corner of the couch, pulling my booted foot up. "I've been reviewing my notes, trying to figure out who killed Sylvia and why. I remembered something

Charlene said from the day you, Hazel, and I met with her at the coffee shop."

He stared at the ceiling. "We told her we were sorry about her mom, and she told us Roger Keaton was her dad." He glanced at me. "That part?"

"Nope. The part where she said it was her mom's love of birding that caused all the problems." I leaned forward, my hand resting on his. "I'm thinking rivalry. Sylvia, Marla, and Estelle Keaton were in the military—"

He interrupted me. "Yes, the Navy. I checked into it."

"So what causes rivalry among women?" I held up my hand and counted off on three fingers. "It's men, work, and according to Charlene, something to do with birding." I handed Hazel's notebook to Shortie. "I'm trying to figure out the connection between the three women. That's where the answer is, I'm sure of it."

"Can I borrow a pen?"

I grabbed one from the coffee table and handed it to him. "What are you going to do?"

He drew arrows from the women's names to the possible rivalry aspects. Next to Marla's name, he put Neil Braden in parenthesis with an arrow from his name to Sylvia's. He did the same with Estelle, writing Roger Keaton next to hers and another arrow to Sylvia. He tapped Sylvia's name with the end of the pen. "She's what everything comes back to."

"Yes, as far as men. She had an affair with both men. And Charlene is Keaton's daughter. But that doesn't get us anywhere." I raised my hands. "We are missing something. Hazel wondered when Sylvia's funeral would be." I batted my eyelashes. "Could you call her and ask?"

Shortie laughed. "Sure." He fished his phone from his pocket and called Charlene's number, putting the cell on speaker.

"What can I do for you?" Her tone, a bit frosty, surprised me.

Is she mad? I mouthed.

He shrugged. "I wanted to check on you. See how you're doing. And ask when your mother's funeral will be. We'd like to pay our respects. The birders, I mean." He stumbled over his last words.

Charlene sighed. "I'm sorry. People keep bothering me. Asking me questions. The police have come by my house again. Dad is in Guatemala, and Estelle is no help. I've never planned anything like this before." Her voice trembled.

"It's not something we practice for," he agreed. "Can we help?"

"No. No, it's fine. I think I've figured it out. I've set a date for Monday evening, and we'll have a celebration of her life. Because it's a murder investigation ..." She sniffled. "Because of how she died, we won't get her ashes for a few weeks." She blew her nose in a loud honk.

"What time is the service and where?" Shortie grabbed the pen and scribbled the information on a fresh sheet of paper. "Thank you, Charlene. I think most of the birders will attend."

They said their goodbyes, and he clicked off the call. "Let the birding group know and encourage everyone to come. Can they all meet here on Monday? Before the celebration of life? We can hand out assignments."

I smirked. "You're coming around to my side, I see."

"I was always on your side." He winked.

Chapter 20

Monday afternoon, I picked up Hazel from Chloe's and stopped for pizzas on the way home. The birders were coming over for an early supper before Sylvia's celebration of life, and we wanted to talk about the investigation. I'd set the food on the island and pulled down paper plates and napkins when there was a knock on my front door.

"Come on in," I hollered.

Shortie entered, shut the door behind him, and cocked an eyebrow.

"What?"

He grinned. "Just thinking how pretty you are."

This was another side of the man I thought I knew. Heat warmed my cheeks, and I stifled my own smile. "You're sweet."

"It's true. What can I do to help."

I handed him the paper plates and napkins. "Set these out, please. People can grab what they like here on the island. Everyone else should arrive soon." I lined the pizzas up, tops propped open.

Hazel came into the room, and she hugged Shortie. "I was

putting my things away. I think Chloe's fine, so I'll stay home after tonight."

"It's not even been a full week," I said.

She flapped her hand. "I was in their way. They have their routines, and Chloe is doing well. No more bleeding. She has an OB appointment on Wednesday. If I have to, I'll go back."

This would put a damper on my and Shortie's budding "more than a friendship." He winked, and I relaxed. None of this needed to go fast. We weren't on a timeline.

"That works." I surveyed the kitchen and dining area. "Anything else we need?"

"I don't think so." Hazel peeked into Roscoe's cage. "Hey, buddy," she cooed. She stuck her finger through the bars. "How's my Roscoe?"

He fluttered his wings. "Birds alive!" he screeched.

She rocked back on her heels. "Where in the world did he learn that, Peg?" Hands on hips, she glared at me, the normal sparkle in her eyes gone. "I've never heard that expression except when we were on the phone."

"I don't know." And that was true. I didn't. I assumed the intruder said it, but I had no proof.

A knock on the front door interrupted us, and Owen stuck his head inside. "We're here." Carmen and Marla followed him in.

Everyone grabbed their pizza of choice and a water bottle, and we settled in the living room. I'd set some chairs around with little TV trays beside them so we could all fit. Shortie sat beside me on the couch, Hazel on his other side. It tickled me to watch Carmen eat the gooey, cheese pizza—dainty pinky finger in the air and all. I'd come to care about my fellow birders and their quirks.

"So, what's the plan for tonight?" Owen asked, licking pizza sauce from his thumb.

Shortie and I discussed this beforehand. Marla remained on our list of suspects, so we needed to be careful what we said. I'd also told him Hazel wasn't aware of the break-in at my house.

So many conversational landmines.

"We want to pay our respects." I set my food on my plate and sipped from my water bottle. I screwed the top back on. "We're also keeping an eye out for an orange license plate on a black sedan."

Hazel piped up. "It says, 'woman veteran.'" She turned to Marla. "Were you in the military?"

Marla choked before clearing her throat. "Yes."

Shortie, Hazel, and I leaned forward, waiting for more information.

Marla wiped her mouth on her napkin and twisted off the top of her water bottle. After a long drink, she put the lid on and picked up her pizza again.

"What branch were you in?" Carmen asked.

The three of us let out simultaneous sighs and sat back. If the situation weren't so intense, I would've laughed.

"My husband was in the Army," Carmen continued. She wiped her fingers with her napkin and stood. "Peg, want me to dump this in the trashcan?"

"Yes, of course." I waved my hand. We'd gotten off track. "Were you in the Army, Marla?"

She chewed and swallowed. "Mm-hmm. Navy."

"I'm retired Navy." Shortie elbowed me. "I was an MP."

Marla offered no other information. Time for a direct approach.

"You told us you knew Sylvia. Was she in the Navy?" I asked.

"You should ask her daughter tonight." She stood, wiped

her hands, and threw her trash away. "I'm going to head over to the funeral home. Y'all know where it is, right?"

"Yep, the one off of Highway 90. Not far from Sylvia's house," Shortie said.

Marla nodded, waved, and rushed out.

"That didn't work like we thought it would," I whispered.

Owen checked his watch. "Should we get going too? The celebration of life starts in half an hour."

Carmen followed him out while Shortie helped put the pizza away, and I straightened up the kitchen.

Shortie slipped CB some crust and then pulled the trash bag closed. "I'll stick this in the can outside, or you know who"—he tipped his head at the dog—"might get into it."

I shook out a new bag and tucked it into the can. "Thanks. I think everything is put away. Can Hazel and I ride with you?"

"Yep."

We followed him out the front door, Shortie stuck the trash in the can, and we all climbed into his vehicle. The humidity was high, causing my dress to cling to my back. I sighed with relief when the air conditioner kicked on.

Hazel buckled her seat belt. "Marla sure acted funny."

"I agree." Shortie put his arm on the back of my seat and reversed out of my driveway. He squeezed my shoulder before shifting into drive. "I wonder if the police will be there tonight. Considering they probably think the killer may show up too."

Ugh. He was warning me Marcus might be at the funeral home. My feelings about him were so mixed up. How could one little kiss from Shortie change my mind about Marcus? It wasn't just that, though. Marcus had shown another side of him in how he reacted with Shortie. I couldn't stand unkindness or disrespect. Zack was never like that, and I wasn't going to lower my standards. Especially after growing up seeing my dad that way with my mom. My opinion of Marcus dropped several notches. I thought of him comparing himself to Shortie. Shortie's side would be higher on the scale now.

Tonight's focus was learning more about Sylvia's life and trying to discover who killed her. I told Shortie and Hazel that, adding to myself that I wanted to find out who had broken into my house. Hazel still didn't need to know that had happened. Not yet. I wasn't ready to answer her questions or have her be frightened.

We parked beside the funeral home. The building sat close to Scenic Highway with the cemetery to its side and extending back for acres and acres.

"This place is huge." I climbed from my seat and helped Hazel down.

"I read it's fifty-seven acres." Shortie took my hand, Hazel walking on my other side. "Barrancas is almost twice the acreage."

I waited for him to hold open the front door of the building. "Wow. I wonder where Sylvia will be buried."

"Ms. Newman's memorial service is this way." The funeral director greeted us at the door and spoke in a hushed tone, waving us to the room on the right.

"Do we all need to whisper?" I whispered.

"Hush and behave." Shortie squeezed my hand and kissed my cheek.

I covered my smile and looked up, straight into Marcus's eyes, thankful Shortie hadn't seen him yet. My cheeks warmed, but I held my head high. The police were there to watch for the killer, like we were.

We joined Carmen and Owen at the back of the room and walked by pictures displayed on the tables. Framed photos of Sylvia and Charlene, Sylvia and birds, and Sylvia by herself were everywhere. I turned and surveyed the rest of the attendees.

"Marla isn't here."

Shortie turned. "What?"

"Marla. She's not here. She left my house before we did. Before Owen."

"Huh. Maybe she's in the ladies' room?"

"I'll check." I hurried out of the room and up the hall. I found the restroom just past a storage closet and opened the door. "Marla? Are you in here?"

A toilet flushed, and Charlene emerged from a stall. She turned on the water and pumped soap into her hands. "It's only me in here." She rinsed her hands, dried them on a paper towel, and used the backs of her index fingers to blot under her eyes. "How do I look?" She stood tall, smoothing down her skirt. "Estelle is here, and she intimidates me."

Her comment surprised me. She didn't know me well enough for her to confide in me. "You're fine. Your mother just died. It's okay if you cry."

She blinked rapidly, inhaled, and exhaled hard. "No, it's not. I have to be on point to survive the dragon stepmother."

Oh boy. Not what I expected her to say. I held the door and followed her out. "I didn't realize you didn't have a good relationship with her."

She stopped, and I had to step to the side to avoid running into her. "You need to check her out. I think she was involved with my mother's death." Her voice, although low, was grave and harsh.

I opened my mouth to ask more questions when the funeral director approached.

He touched her shoulder and leaned forward, speaking in his funereal voice. "Ms. Newman, it's time to begin."

Charlene straightened her shoulders and marched off.

Once again, I followed in her wake. I spotted the birders sitting together several rows back from the podium, and I joined them, slipping into the aisle seat beside Shortie.

He leaned over. "Did you find Marla?"

"No sign of her, but Charlene told me we need to keep an eye on Estelle."

The pastor leading the service stood and asked us to bow our heads to pray, cutting short our conversation. Shortie put his arm around me and bowed his head by mine.

After the prayer, Charlene was introduced. She spoke about her mother with no tears in sight. While she talked, I read the small funeral program. It had a picture of Sylvia on the front with her birth and death dates. Inside, it showed the order of the service on one side and an obituary on the other. I tuned out Charlene's words and read:

"Sylvia Newman grew up in Pensacola and was a birder from a young age. She graduated from Woodham High School in 1978 and entered the U.S. Navy through the Delayed Entry Program with her best friends, Estelle Keaton and Marla Braden. She worked alongside her friends at Naval Air Station Pensacola in the administration building for four years before she left the service.

Ms. Newman was the first to report the rufous hummingbird in Pensacola. She received local and national recognition for finding the vagrant bird. She lived for birding and was always searching for the next rare bird.

In lieu of flowers, her daughter requests donations be made to the Audubon Society."

I elbowed Shortie. "What is a vagrant bird?"

Hazel shushed me, but I held out the program for Shortie.

He pointed to the front of the room. "Listen."

Charlene told a funny story about her mother and birds

and explained what Sylvia had done when she discovered the rufous hummingbird.

"If you don't know, over 350 species of hummingbirds live in the United States. The rufous was found in the northwestern part of the United States. That is a long way from northwest Florida. Mother spotted the first rufous hummingbird in Florida in the early '80s—the winter before I was born. From her stories, she told all the right people and threw a 'bird-spotting' party in her backyard." She made air quotes.

She wrapped up her reminiscing, and someone sang a sad song. I listened with half my mind—the other half whirring with information about birds and dates.

I elbowed Shortie again. "What if when Charlene said birding caused all the problems, she meant this rufous bird thing."

This time he shushed me. The pastor had called for us to bow our heads again. Afterward, he invited everyone to Sylvia's house for refreshments.

Hazel leaned across Shortie. "We have to go. I haven't discovered anything here."

"Me either." I followed her and Shortie outside. Marcus wasn't in sight, but sirens blared down Scenic Highway. I didn't see the black sedan or Estelle anywhere.

Owen caught up with us. "I'm going to drop Carmen off at your house, Peg, to get her car. Neither of us feels up to going for refreshments."

"No problem. Did you spot anyone suspicious?"

"No, and I think we need to let the police find the killer."

"I understand." I hugged him, waved to Carmen, and climbed into the Jeep.

"That is one good-looking man," Hazel said.

I turned in my seat. "I thought you said you don't need a man?"

She fanned her face. "Yes, I did. I don't. But he is quite handsome. Don't you think?"

I chuckled at Shortie's face—eyebrow cocked, worried expression. "Hmm. Owen's a little old for me." I glanced at Hazel again. "Just your age." I sat back and tapped my chin. "I think you should go for it."

She poked my shoulder. "Let's keep our minds on this murder business for now. I'll think about Owen after."

Shortie parked off to the side of Sylvia's drive. Police cars, lights flashing, sat in the driveway. "What's going on? I thought we were here for refreshments?"

Hazel shoved open her car door. "I don't know, but let's go find out."

We headed for the front door, which hung open. This reminded me too much of when I had found Sylvia wounded and dying. Goosebumps broke out on my arms, and I shivered. Memories of that day flashed in my mind. I stopped in my tracks.

"What's up?" Shortie rubbed my back.

I inhaled, attempting to calm my racing heart. "It's just …"

"Was the door open when you found her?"

I nodded and drew another deep breath.

"Hang on, Hazel," he said. "Stay with Peg, and I'll check this out."

Hazel waited on the front walk with me. More mourners from the service had gathered where we stood. It didn't take long before Shortie rejoined us.

"What happened?" I asked.

He leaned in and lowered his voice. "Marla is inside. The house is a mess."

"Marla?" Hazel forgot to lower her voice, and the others in the group crowded closer.

"What happened?"

"Can we go in?"

"Why are the police here?"

Questions rang out, and Shortie held out both hands, lowering them in a hushing motion. "Quiet down, quiet down. There was a break-in at Ms. Newman's. I would suggest everyone go home."

Charlene appeared in the doorway. "Please do what Mr. Jackson has asked." She fluttered her hands toward the driveway. "Thank you for your kindness." Her shoulders slumped, and she turned to reenter the house.

I hurried forward, Hazel and Shortie on my heels. "Charlene, what can we do?"

She groaned, her chin dropping to her chest. "I don't know. Someone got into the house, and Marla is hurt."

"What?" Hazel squawked.

"That's what I didn't want to tell them." Shortie thumbed over his shoulder. He grabbed my arm. "They think she interrupted a break-in. She's unconscious."

My vision blurred, and stars filled my sight. I grabbed Shortie's arm. "I don't feel so good."

Next thing I knew, I woke up on the couch in Sylvia's living room.

Chapter 21

I pushed up to sit, and Hazel rushed over and handed me a wet washcloth.

She propped a pillow behind me. "How are you?"

"I don't know." A glance around Sylvia's living room showed it was a wreck. Food had been knocked off catering tables and trays. Folding chairs that had been set out for visitors had been pushed over. "Where is Marla? What happened in here?"

Hazel patted my shoulder. "They took her out to the ambulance. Use the cloth now, Peg."

I stared at the rag she had handed me. She took it from my hand and laid it across the back of my neck.

"Thank you," I whispered.

A female EMT stepped into the room. "Ma'am? How are you? Mr. Jackson said you fainted and asked me to check you out."

I snorted. Fainted? Me? "I'm okay." My words sounded weak to my ears. I cleared my throat and tried again. "I'm fine."

Hazel flapped her hand. "Check her over, please. She found Sylvia when she died here. This is too much for her."

My hands trembled, and another shiver ran through me. I hated being so frail.

The EMT took my pulse and blood pressure and examined my head. "When you fell, did you hit your head?" She checked my pupils.

"I don't remember?"

Hazel piped up. "Shortie caught her and brought her in here."

I blushed. Besides the fact I fainted, I now knew Shortie had carried me into Sylvia's. I buried my face in my hands.

"Ma'am?" The EMT tapped my shoulder. "Ma'am? What hurts?"

"Just my ego. I'm all right." I grimaced.

"Mr. Jackson took good care of you. Sit here for a bit, though, until you feel steady." She put her medical gear away and left the room.

"Hazel," I said, leaning against her. "Can we sneak out the back?" I didn't want to see Shortie. Not yet.

She laughed and patted my knee. "Don't be embarrassed. When you're ready, we'll go home."

"How is Marla? She's not dead, is she?" I didn't add the word *too*. I just couldn't.

"She was injured, but she's alive." She waved toward the room and explained what she'd learned from listening in on the police conversation. "The caterers were gone when Marla stopped by, but when they came back, someone rushed out of the house. They came inside to this mess and found her."

"Who would do that? Break in here?"

"I don't know, but often burglars read the obits and target houses that might be empty. It sure sounds suspicious to me, though. Too many things have happened here."

Like Sylvia dying and me getting pushed. And fainting. Ugh. I shifted on the couch and propped my boot on the glass coffee table. It wouldn't make a difference with the destruction that had happened.

"I wonder if Marla knows who attacked her?" Hazel said.

"I don't think I'm up for any investigating right now." I yawned. My adrenaline had left, leaving me exhausted.

"I'm sending you home with Shortie. I'll get a ride from someone."

Home sounded wonderful. Once the police didn't need us and I stopped shaking, Shortie helped me into his car, started the engine, and headed for the interstate. I turned as we drove off and spotted Marcus standing in Sylvia's doorway. The sun was setting, and his face was in the shadows. I tried to shake off the doom consuming me.

"I cannot believe someone attacked Marla," I said. "And that Sylvia's house was burglarized."

"And you fainted." Shortie reached over and squeezed my hand.

"Yeah. Thanks for taking care of me."

"Anytime."

I wasn't planning on fainting again anytime soon or ever, but I liked knowing someone was looking out for me— someone besides a friend or family. Zack's face crossed my mind and faded. It was like he was telling me it was time. Time for me. I could let him go. I tightened my grip on Shortie's hand.

He blew out a breath and tapped the steering wheel with his free hand. "It's crazy what happened. I tried to find out details, but all they'd tell me was Marla must have interrupted the intruder."

"Hazel thinks she stopped at Sylvia's on the way to the funeral home." I paused. "Or, she never intended to go to the celebration of life." A thought occurred to me, and I turned to Shortie. "I bet she went to find the emails and letters. We never told her we had them." My shoulders slumped. The information might have prevented Marla from getting hurt."

Shortie pulled to the side of the road and took me in his arms. "This is not your fault or Hazel's. It isn't. Say it."

"It's not my fault," I mumbled, snuggling into his embrace.

He pulled back and cocked an eyebrow. "I mean it. Marla was a suspect, remember? She wasn't the intruder. Someone else was in the house." He held me closer before letting go and pulling back into traffic.

"Yeah, that's not encouraging."

Shortie dropped me at my house, and with CB by his side, he checked all the rooms and the garage. He opened the back door blinds and flipped the light on. "When is the insurance adjustor coming about the tree?"

I joined him at the sliding door. "They're supposed to be here as soon as possible. I'm sure other people had worse damage."

"True. But it's been two weeks." He slid his arm around my waist. We stood together for several moments before he heaved a sigh.

"You okay?"

"I am." He brushed my hair back. "I need to leave."

"All right." I took another step back, my heart plunging. I didn't think he would play games with my feelings.

He caught my hands and pulled me closer. "It's not that I want to, Peg." His eyes darkened, and a smile tipped the corner of his mouth. "It's dark, it's late, we're alone." He grimaced. "I gotta go." Shortie squeezed my hands and leaned in for a quick kiss. "You all right until Hazel comes back?"

My pulse had ratcheted up, and I was sure my neck and face blazed dark red. "Yes, I'll be fine. I have CB and Roscoe." I winked.

"Pensacola's finest, for sure." Shortie kissed my cheek and headed for the front door. "Lock this behind me."

I saluted him, and he chuckled.

"Night, Peg."

After I turned the deadbolt behind him, I watched him leave through the blinds, rubbing my arms against a shiver from his words and kiss. The Jeep's taillights disappeared as Shortie rounded the corner—time to get ready for bed.

EARLY THE NEXT MORNING, my phone rang. I stumbled out to the kitchen, hobbling on my sore ankle. I'd removed the boot and hadn't put it back on for the day yet.

"Yes, who is this?" I swiped my hair out of my face.

"Good morning to you, too." Marcus's sarcastic response made me frown.

"Hi. Sorry. I just woke up." I grabbed a paper towel and wet it. I set my cell on the kitchen counter and rubbed my face. Mumbling came from the phone. I pushed the speaker button. "Hey, can you repeat what you said?"

"Marla Braden is at the hospital. She has bruises and a slight concussion. I thought you'd want to know."

"Oh my. Thank you. What happened yesterday? Do you have more details?" I tilted the blinds open over the sink and limped into the dining area to sit.

"It's an investigation, Peg. I can't divulge that information." His tone was flat.

Why did he call me then? "So, you called to tell me about Marla?"

He grunted. "Yes. No." He sighed. "Did something happen to you? I heard you passed out."

"Fainted."

"Same thing." His smirk came through the phone line. "So? You okay?"

"Shortie caught me and carried me inside." Yes, I was rubbing salt in the wound, but he wouldn't tell me what happened—seemed fair to me.

"Got it. Glad he was there. Talk later." He hung up.

"Men," I muttered. Someone knocked at my front door. "Hang on," I hollered. More hobbling. I peeped through the peephole and unlocked the door to find Lauree on my porch.

She tipped her head, eyebrows pulled up. "Just wake up?"

"How can you tell?" I held the corners of my PJ top out and curtsied. "Give me a minute to dress and brush my teeth."

"I'll start the coffee," she said.

I slipped into jeans and a lightweight flannel, brushed my teeth and hair, and grabbed my boot and tennis shoe. The aroma of coffee brewing made my mouth water, and I limped into the kitchen.

"Mmm. I love coffee." I sat and pulled on the boot and the shoe.

She poured coffee into two mugs, handing me one, and joined me at the bar. She pointed to my boot. "How is your ankle?"

I wiggled it back and forth. "It's a little better, but it's only been two weeks. I think my follow-up is late October."

"Girl, it seems like longer than two weeks." Lauree sipped her coffee. She tapped her fingers on the island countertop.

Something was bothering her, and I wasn't sure I would like it. "What's up?"

She swiveled her barstool to face me. "I'm worried. About you."

"Why?" I couldn't think of anything she would be worried about. Murder and break-ins notwithstanding.

She bit her lip. "I don't know how to say this."

I sipped my coffee. "Spit it out, please. Before I start worrying about me."

"Was Shortie here last night?" Her words rushed out. The concern on her face made me smile.

"Yes, Mother. He took me to Sylvia's celebration of life and brought me home after I fainted."

She clutched my hand. "You fainted? Good gracious, Peg. This is ridiculous."

"Are you mad at me?"

"I'm scared for you. You ... you were interested in Marcus just the other day, and now Shortie is bringing you home. And you fainted?"

I leaned forward and hugged her. "You are my best friend," I whispered in her ear. "Where would I be without you."

She swiped a tear from her cheek. "I don't know. For years, you've lived here, and we've had Mamma Birds. Now you have new friends and these men." Her mouth twisted when she said "men." "I know, I know. It's been years since Zack died. You deserve to find love. I'm just ..." She pinched her lips together and sniffled. "I miss you. I miss us." She gestured between us.

I held onto her again and let her cry. She sat back and hiccupped.

"I'm sorry." She fanned her face. "I'm hormonal."

"Hormonal?" I peered at my friend. Her cheeks were covered in a faint rash, and she had acne on her chin. "PMS hormonal?" I cocked an eyebrow.

"I think so? Maybe I'm pregnant." She laughed at my expression. "Kidding! I'm kidding. I promise."

"You had me going there for a second! Seriously, though, I'm fine. Yes, I thought Marcus might be the guy, but he showed his true colors. Nothing awful, just too cocky for me. Too much like my dad."

She made a face. "You told me about him. I'm sorry things worked out that way with Marcus. What about Shortie?"

Heat crawled up my neck. "Yeah, Shortie. He's the guy. For sure. I mean, I think so. He's pretty amazing." I propped my chin on my palm and tipped my head to her. "It's not too soon, is it? I mean Zack died thirteen years ago."

I'd never thought about another man until now. When Zack first died, I stayed busy raising the kids. And until Carter moved out, my blog took up all my time. It was the empty nest that did it. I thought back to the quote I'd read a month ago. My nest may be empty, but my life was full now, and I liked it.

"No, I'm happy for you. I just worried you were jumping too fast."

"Thirteen years *is* fast," I deadpanned.

"Funny girl. Now, why did you faint?"

I brought her up to speed, and she asked me more questions about Shortie. I assured her we were going slow and being careful.

"He even left last night after he checked the house. Hazel wasn't home yet, and he was uncomfortable we were alone."

"He respects you. I like that." She nodded her approval. "Is Hazel here? Have you seen her yet today?"

"No. She must be sleeping in."

Lauree hesitated, and then said, "I have one other thing I want to talk to you about. Alone."

I stood and got the coffee pot, pouring us both another mugful before sitting again. "What is it?"

She studied her cup, turning it in circles on the counter. "Well, I've taken over a good bit of the blog like you and I discussed. And ... I was thinking ... would you be interested in selling Mamma Birds to me?"

Chapter 22

I gulped. Selling Mamma Birds to anyone was something I'd never thought about. I still remembered the day I told Lauree about starting my blog. Mom blogs were catching on, and I figured it was a skill I had—writing—and a topic I knew about—mommying. So I invested a small amount of Zack's life insurance money in my website and learned everything I could about blogging. My following grew—I think my readers liked the play on words—Mamma Birds. Lauree was a great cheerleader, and within a few years, she became my social media manager.

"We make a good team," I said.

"I know, we do," Lauree said. "I love doing more behind the scenes and contributing blog posts."

"And?" I prompted, grabbing her coffee mug and setting it to the side to keep her from playing with it.

She pursed her lips. "You said you didn't relate with the young moms anymore."

I did say that. And that's why I started the Empty Nesters Birding Group, which would never support me financially. So far, all that had happened was people had died.

A small voice in my head reminded me of Shortie and my friendships with Owen and Carmen.

I closed my eyes and prayed.

"Peg?"

"I need to think about this, okay? It's a big step."

Lauree leaned over and wrapped her arms around me. "I understand. I hope you're not mad. It's just something I've been thinking about."

"I'm not mad, I promise. If anyone took over the blog, I'd want it to be you. But it's a lot to consider."

After she left I sat at the bar, still stunned by her question. Give up Mamma Birds? I hadn't paid it much attention in the last couple of weeks, but I wasn't ready to sell it. At least I didn't think so. I still earned a steady income from advertising, sponsorships, and my shop.

All the things that had happened recently ran through my mind. Anna's and Sylvia's deaths and finding the killer. My broken foot. The hurricane and damage to my house. Hazel and her animals. Lauree's question about buying my blog. Marcus and Shortie. My brain stopped at Shortie. He had become a friend, and I could maybe see a future with him. But I had to lay down my love for Zack.

Or did I?

I grabbed my cell and texted Shortie.

Can you chat?

He answered right away, and we decided to meet at a Greek restaurant for lunch. Their gyros were good, but their spanakopita was my favorite. My stomach rumbled just thinking about the spinach pie with feta and layered phyllo.

Right now, breakfast called. Half a bagel went well with my coffee, and as I finished my last bite, Hazel came out of her room.

"Good morning. You slept late."

She rubbed her eyes. "I think you got up early. Who was at the door?"

My shoulders slumped. "Lauree."

"What's wrong?" She got a mug, poured the hot brew, and stirred in a teaspoon of sugar. She sat beside me at the bar with a quizzical expression.

"She asked to buy Mamma Birds from me."

"What?" Hazel's screech sparked Roscoe to holler, "Birds alive!" and CB to bark repeatedly.

Her brow wrinkled. She'd asked me several times where Roscoe had learned his new saying. I could truthfully say I didn't know. But I had my suspicions.

This time, she didn't ask.

"Yeah, I told her I have to think about it. And I've never checked into any kind of service for Anna." I plopped my chin in my hand. Today was one of those days. The kind where the skies felt a little lower, and the darkest cloud hovered over my head. I hummed, "I'm just a little black rain cloud."

She elbowed me. "Quit that. You have a terrific life." She leaned back and pointed to herself. "You have me as a roommate."

I chuckled and sat up. "You're right. And I'm meeting Shortie for lunch." I wiggled my eyebrows.

"Ooh la la!" Her eyes sparkled.

"Well, we're going to Founaris Brothers. How do you say that in Greek?"

SHORTIE WAS WAITING inside the restaurant when I arrived. A waitress showed us to a booth in the back, handed us menus, and started on the list of specials.

I handed the menu back. "I know what I want."

"Me too," Shortie said.

"Spanakopita," we chorused.

While we waited for our food, I toyed with the paper from my straw. Shortie captured my hand, removing the paper and balling it up. He pushed it to the side and reached for my other hand.

"I'm glad you asked me to lunch."

Heat climbed my neck. I'd asked him on a date. My stomach roiled. But I reminded myself this was Shortie, and my stomach settled. I squeezed his hands.

"This is a big deal for me."

"I know."

"I'm not positive I'm ready." I had to be honest.

"I know."

I chuckled. "You know a lot."

His thumb rubbed the back of my hand. "I like you, Peg. I really do. I think we could, you know …"

This time I said, "I know."

That broke the ice for me. Realizing he cared about my feelings and understood this was a new thing for me— lightness and tension flowed out of my body. I didn't need to talk to him about letting go of Zack. I would work through that on my own.

"Lauree came over today," I said.

He leaned back for the waitress to set our food down and then said a short prayer. He took a bite of his food. "So good."

"Anything with feta is good, but this is the best." I picked up my garlic bread.

"So tell me why Lauree came over."

I finished my bite of bread and sipped my soda. "She asked about buying Mamma Birds from me."

His eyebrows shot up. "Mamma Birds? What's that?"

"My blog. My mom blog. It's … kind of a big thing?" I couldn't believe he'd never heard of it.

"That's cool. I didn't know you blogged."

"It's how I make my living." I waited for the metaphorical shoe to drop.

He stopped mid-chew. "You make money from it?"

"Yep." I dug into my side salad, enjoying the emotions playing across his face. It dawned on me one of the things I loved about Zack was how I knew what he was feeling because of his expressions. I liked that about Shortie too. What you saw was what you got.

He leaned forward. "You make a living from it? From blogging? On a blog?" He blinked and scratched his head. "How?"

"Well, I worked really hard. It's been going on for about thirteen years. Since Zack died."

"But you're just writing, right? Like, how do you make money off of that?"

I waved my fork in the air. "Advertising, sponsors, I make printables for moms, stuff like that."

He sat back. "You are amazing. You know that?"

"I know."

Shortie helped me hash out the pros and cons of selling my blog. He wrote them on a napkin so I could read through them and add whatever I thought of. I explained it was like giving up one of my kids. I *was* Mamma Birds.

I showed Hazel the list when I got home. As hard as it was to imagine, she had become a good friend and a trusted confidante.

She pointed to the napkin. "Fancy stationary."

"Thanks."

"So, go through each side for me."

We sat on the couch, and I pointed to the pros column. "First, I'm not a young mom anymore."

Hazel frowned. "Lauree's your age."

"Almost. But she had her kids later in life. She relates to having young kids, elementary school kids. I don't. Not really. I remember the life, but honestly? It's kind of a blur now."

"I get that. I told Chloe back in my day, we didn't have Lamaze or natural childbirth."

I imitated Lamaze breathing. "You never did that?"

"Nope."

"You aren't that old." I grabbed my phone and researched natural childbirth online. "Hah, you are lying! The Lamaze method was around when I was born."

Hazel winked and swatted me with a couch pillow. "Don't tell Chloe. You'll ruin my reputation."

We both giggled, and then she pointed to the list. "What's next?"

"I had problems coming up with more positives for selling. Besides the fact I am selling my dream, it's just such a part of me."

"Is it really your dream, Peg?"

"What do you mean?" Her question stopped me in my tracks.

She launched into a long and involved discourse on dreams and how women need to think big, allow themselves to change plans as their lives changed, and not stop doing it. I had no idea she thought about all of those things. When she wound down, she repeated her question, "Is Mamma Birds really your dream?"

I had to answer no. Tears welled and trickled down my face. Truthfully, Mamma Birds hatched from a need. I needed to be home with my kids, and blogging gave me a way to do that and provide an income.

"I'm not sure what my dream is." I sniffled and wiped my cheeks.

She patted my hand. "I'll help you. We'll figure it out. Like I said, dreams can change through your life. Through the different stages. You're an empty nester now, not a young mom."

"Thanks, I think?" I stuck my tongue out at her. But I knew what she meant.

She hurried to her room, returned with her notebook, and flipped to an empty page. "We still have to solve Sylvia's murder, but let's work on you for now."

She handed me the paper and a pen and told me to write down the things I liked to do, explaining those were some of my gifts and could be used in deciding what I wanted to do.

"Gifts from God," she said and nodded as if that sealed everything.

And it did. As I wrote what I enjoyed doing and ranked them, I found I was good at blogging and writing and especially wanted to help people.

I tapped the page. "That makes sense because I'm happiest when I create lists and printables for moms. Things that help them organize."

Hazel tipped her head. "Do you really make a full-time income from blogging?"

"Yep."

She mentioned a well-known mommy blogger. "Do you make more than her? She's been around for a long time."

"She started about five years before me. She got in on the ground floor of mom blogs. To answer your question, yes, I make more than her, I think."

Her mouth dropped open. "I had no idea."

"We don't share income, but I know several big-name sponsorships and advertisers dropped her when she declared her firm opinions on breastfeeding versus bottle feeding and cloth versus disposable diapers."

Hazel was speechless.

I shrugged. "It's true. They came to me and offered me a contract. I don't like to tell moms what to do. I like to give them options. Their kids aren't mine to raise."

"Wow. You had to do a lot of learning."

"A ton. You know what, I wonder if I could still blog." I scribbled some more things I enjoyed doing and pointed to them. "What do you think? Any way to combine these?"

Lauree and I arranged to meet the next morning. We chose a café on Nine Mile. It opened after another restaurant at the same location closed, and I still hadn't had a chance to go there. Lauree said they had chicken and waffles, and I wanted to see if they were as good as the ones Zack and I had eaten when we went to Memphis for our honeymoon years ago.

Zack. Another decision. Not right now, though. First, I was going to find out what I could about Anna.

When I texted the remaining original birders—Owen, Carmen, and Shortie—and asked if any of them knew Anna's last name, Owen responded he thought it was Thompson. I searched the obits online for Anna Thompson and finally found a small write-up about her. She had no children, spouse, or scheduled service, just a bare-bones obituary. Who put the announcement in then?

I picked up my cell again and called the *Pensacola News Journal*, asking for the obituary department. When an employee answered, I explained what I needed.

"No idea, ma'am. It doesn't show a contact person."

"Don't you require that?" I asked.

"All I can tell you is that there isn't one. Someone must have dropped the ball."

"Okay, thanks." Someone dropped the ball all right, but who? I hung up. No way to find that out since none of us had any other information on her. A glance at my watch showed it was time to go meet Lauree. I grabbed my things and headed out in my SUV.

When I arrived at the café, I reminded myself this was my best friend. Lauree waved from a booth near the back of the room. Good. I didn't want to be by the door and be interrupted by people walking in. She and I needed to talk. Really talk.

I still wasn't sure what I would say to her. The openings I'd prepared weren't how she and I communicated. I set my purse on the chair next to me and watched her bite her lip and fiddle with her napkin and silverware. I put my hand over hers.

"Our friendship will not change. We will always be besties."

Tears streamed down her cheeks, and she smiled through them. "You're too old to say 'besties.'"

"BFFs, then?"

She swallowed. "Thank you. I worried all night. Afraid I had ruined our friendship. That you would hate what I asked."

"No, no. Listen,"—I grabbed her hand and held on tight—"I have an idea. Well, Hazel helped me come up with it, but I think it's good."

Chapter 23

When I explained what I was thinking—that I would start a whole section on our blog for empty nesters—Lauree's eyes lit up.

"That is the best idea," she squealed. "And bringing Chloe on board for first-time moms—brilliant."

I spread my napkin on my lap and picked up the menu. "All Hazel's ideas. When I told her you and I had talked about where I am in life, she suggested covering all the bases."

Lauree fanned her face. "I'm so excited. And relieved." She huffed out a big sigh. "I was really worried you would be mad. But you creating the older mom slash empty nester part of the blog will be right up your alley. And it will extend our reach."

Our waitress stopped, passed out two glasses of ice water, and poured coffee into thick, white cups. After she took our order, I sipped my coffee. "I don't know why, but coffee in these mugs tastes so good." I drank more.

"Fresh and hot." Lauree wiped her mouth with her napkin. "When do you want to integrate your part of the blog?"

We discussed how to split the blog into three parts and headings. I hadn't approached Chloe yet, but I thought she would want to contribute to and lead a section for new moms. We hashed out details on ads, sponsorships, and money and agreed we needed a lawyer to draw up a contract. Neither of us wanted money to divide our friendship.

"I think we should start my section as soon as possible. And the transition from my first post about wanting a new hobby will segue nicely to it." I made a face. "We can't call it older moms."

She grimaced. "Yeah, no. That's awful. We could call it empty nesters."

"We can start with that." I fiddled with my coffee mug. "I have another thing I'll probably pursue also."

Lauree glanced up from her menu. "Oh?"

"Maybe I'll write a book. About being an empty nester." I closed my menu and set it on the table. I already knew I wanted chicken and waffles.

She closed hers, too, then tipped her head. "Fiction or non?"

"Nonfiction. Kind of a how-to e-book. I can put it on the website."

"I like that idea!" She slid a napkin toward me. "Got a pen? Let's jot some ideas down."

By the time we finished planning my e-book, I had eaten my chicken and waffles, and Lauree had all but inhaled her seafood omelet. I loved shrimp, but her meal had crawfish too, and I didn't eat those. I forked my last bite of waffles and pointed at her plate.

"Some people call those 'mudbugs.'"

She set her fork across her plate. "They're chopped up in the omelet. It's not like I twisted the head off and sucked the juice out."

"Stop!" I covered my mouth. "Do not say that again."

She giggled. "So ... tell me what's going on with Shortie."

I filled her in on the latest, including our lunch at the Greek restaurant. "He even helped me come up with pros and cons about selling Mamma Birds. Then I asked Hazel what she thought, and she went through this long explanation about dreaming and helped me narrow down what I wanted to do."

She smiled and grabbed my hand. "I have them both to thank. I'm so glad we worked this out. Sounds like you and Shortie are doing well too."

I leaned back in my chair. "Now, we have to find Sylvia's killer."

IT's TOO bad solving a mystery wasn't as easy as picking shoes for birding or deciding what I wanted to be now that I was grown up.

Come to think of it, neither of those was easy either.

As I drove home from breakfast, my brain fired off idea after idea. And all the things I needed to do. Maybe I drank too much coffee?

Nah.

Hazel had taken CB to the doggie park, so it was just me and Roscoe. I tossed him a birdie treat and blew kisses to him. We'd established a tentative relationship. I didn't stick my hand in his cage, and he didn't bite me.

I settled on the couch with my laptop and got to work on my how-to-be-an-empty-nester e-book ideas. Creating with words was my thing, my dream, as I'd discovered when talking to Hazel. It fed my soul and was one way God could use me to help others—my gift from Him.

The only problem was—as I sat there, fingers poised over my keyboard—what came to me was Sylvia's murder, how

Charlene had said birding caused all the problems, the vagrant bird Sylvia discovered, Estelle, and Marla.

"Oh no!" I clapped my hand over my mouth. I never checked on Marla.

A quick text to Marcus answered one of my questions. She was still at West Florida Hospital. I set my laptop aside, grabbed my purse and cell, and headed out.

Marla wasn't a close friend, but she was part of the investigation. And a possible suspect. She'd been at the hospital for almost two days, and this was my chance to talk to her.

I stopped at the welcome desk to get her room number and rode the elevator to her floor. A sign directed me to her room, just to the left of the elevator. I tapped on the door twice and opened it.

"Marla?"

No light shone in her room. The curtains and blinds were pulled tight, and I didn't see any lights from the myriad of monitors situated around her bed.

"Marla? Are you in here?" I stepped back to the light switch by the door.

"Don't do that," growled a husky voice.

"Wh ... what?" I knew that voice. It was my anonymous caller. My body broke out in a sweat, head to toe. "Who are you?"

"You need to leave the room."

Marla groaned, and I snapped into action. I hit the light switch, opened the door, and screamed, "Help!" I didn't know what to do next—go into the room and save Marla or wait for security to come. Quick footsteps sounded behind me, and I turned. A petite, skinny nurse dressed in cartoon character scrubs hurried up the hall.

"Did you call for help? What's going on?" She skidded to a stop and said imperiously, "Who are you?"

I pointed into the room, hand shaking. "They're in there. With her. My anonymous caller."

"What? That doesn't make sense. Who called you? I don't hear anything." She held her hand out. "Can I see your ID, please?"

A sharp thud followed by a moan propelled us to action. As I ran inside Marla's room, I pictured Marcus's face, full of disappointment, followed by Shortie's expression of love and care and worry.

Please keep us safe, Lord. My prayer was short but heartfelt. I entered the room before the nurse and took in the scene in seconds. The same person who had tried to break into Hazel's car at the café in Pace stood over Marla, holding a pillow over her face. At least they were dressed the same way.

The nurse bumped into me, then pushed the call button for emergencies. Lights flashed and blared, and she hollered for more help. The intruder stared at me. He was dressed head-to-toe in black with a ski mask pulled over his face. His eyes were all I could see.

He dropped the pillow and rushed past us. As he passed me, he shoved me into the wall and whispered, "I'll be back for you." His voice, low and still indistinct, caused me to wonder —was this a man or a woman? My head bounced off the wall, and my breath whooshed out.

Who exactly was after Marla, and why?

He ran out the door. Should I follow?

"Is there a stairway?" I asked.

The nurse turned from checking Marla. She pointed. "That way."

I couldn't run with the boot but punched the elevator button and took the first one available. Security ran toward Marla's room as the door slid shut. They'd probably get to the attempted murderer before I could hobble outside, but I wanted to see his car. Maybe I could snap a picture of the license plate number.

My heart pounded on the short elevator ride. Everything had happened in a split second. How did the intruder find Marla?

Bright sunshine blinded me when I stepped from the portico, where cars stopped for valet service. I shielded my eyes and scanned the parking lot while fishing my phone out of my purse with my other hand. Sirens screamed up Davis Highway, heading in my direction. I looked both ways into the crowded parking lot and checked for a black-clothed person or a black sedan.

"I know you're out here," I mumbled. I stepped past the first line of parked cars for a better view of the back row. "Come on now. I don't want to catch you. I just need to see that plate."

A black vehicle, one row up from where I stood, slowly backed out of its spot and turned to exit onto the main road. If that was the car I was searching for, once it hit Davis Highway, I'd never be able to see its tag.

I hobbled as fast as possible and crouched beside a silver van parked two spaces from the car. My phone slipped from my hand and smacked face-down onto the asphalt. "No, no, no." I scooped it up and turned it over. The screen was cracked, but I didn't have time to take a picture anyway.

The sedan was pulling away, and I needed that picture. I glanced up and saw the license plate. As Hazel had shown us on the computer, the plate had an orange background with a female silhouette holding a machine gun. At the bottom were the words—Woman Veteran. But the words on the tag turned my body ice cold.

Brds Aliv.

The sight of the plate and the words I translated as "Birds Alive" burned into my brain and rooted me to where I stood.

In less than a minute, police officers and security guards swarmed the parking lot. Should I stay and tell them what I saw? Or would that get me into trouble? As it was, I knew the nurse would have told them I was a suspicious person or, at the very least, a witness.

My SUV was one row down and half a dozen spots over. I picked my way past the other cars, attempting to stay out of sight. Johnson Avenue, to the right of the hospital, was my destination. As long as the police didn't secure the lot immediately, I could use that to cross over to my neighborhood. Trying to appear casual and unconcerned, I unlocked my car and climbed inside.

If they could see my sweaty, trembling hands, they'd stop and question me. I exhaled hard after turning left onto Johnson and making it through the next traffic light. Marcus and Shortie, with all their questions, popped into my head again, and I groaned. I knew what would happen once that nurse described me with my red hair and a boot on my foot. Not too many women in Pensacola like that.

Ugh.

I rounded the corner onto my street, hit my garage door opener, and drove down the steep driveway, parking beside Hazel's car. In my rearview mirror, I spotted Marcus's cruiser pulling in behind me.

Marcus stood beside my car door when I got out. "Peg." His eyes, dark and cold, bored into mine.

"Hi," I said. "What's up?" I grabbed my purse and entered the house. I was getting better at hobbling quickly. "Hazel?" I needed backup.

He followed me, shutting the door from the garage into the

house and turning the deadbolt. He stopped at the kitchen island, placing both palms flat on it. "Where have you been?"

I worried if he kept grinding his teeth like that, he'd need to see a dentist. Now didn't seem to be the time to mention that.

CB followed Hazel out of her room. The dog licked my hand until I scratched his head. He trotted to Marcus and sat with an expectant expression. Marcus smirked and rubbed the dog's ears.

"Where *have* you been?" Hazel asked me. "CB and I got back half an hour ago, but I didn't see a note saying where you'd gone."

Marcus raised his eyebrows and crossed his arms over his chest, feet planted wide.

I traced the granite pattern on the island. "I went to see Marla at West Florida Hospital."

Hazel perked up. "How is she? Is she feeling better? Did she say anything or know who hurt her?"

Marcus grunted.

"What's wrong?" She looked back and forth between Marcus and me, the furrow between her brows growing. "Peg?" Her tone turned suspicious.

"I didn't see Marla. The lights were off, and before I could turn them on, someone said not to. I turned them on and hollered for help."

Hazel gasped.

"Yes. So like I said, I hollered for help and left the room." I stared at Marcus. "I left the room."

One eyebrow cocked. "Apparently, you re-entered it," he growled.

"No, that was when I first got there. I called for help, a nurse came, and she weighed maybe eighty pounds soaking wet, and we heard noises, and I went in the second time. The person was trying to smother Marla. They dropped the pillow and rushed out. He or she, I really couldn't tell, shoved me into the wall and said they would be back for me. They were dressed like the person who tried to break into your car, Hazel."

My adrenaline faded, my legs quaked, and the blood drained from my head all the way to my toes. "I ... I need to sit."

Marcus grabbed one arm, Hazel the other, and they helped me to the couch. She brought me a glass of water and placed a cool, wet rag on the back of my neck. Marcus stood over me, arms crossed, expression judging my decisions.

I sipped the water, inhaled, exhaled, and waved my hand at Marcus. "Move."

"What?"

If I had the energy, I'd laugh at the childish expression on his face. "Please move. You're making me nervous." I waved him back.

He took one step away but continued glaring. "I heard the call for the incident at the hospital, and somehow I knew it was about you. I headed here, and sure enough, here you are. A redheaded woman wearing an orthopedic boot."

"You're smart. You found me. But guess what I found?"

"What?" Marcus and Hazel asked at the same time.

"The license plate of the person's car. It says, 'Birds Alive.'"

Chapter 24

Roscoe busted out with, "Birds alive! Birds alive!"

Hazel looked at her bird and back to me.

Marcus slapped a hand over his face. "Please tell me you got a picture, make of the car, something." He glared at me through his fingers. "It's probably the same person who broke in here. You know that, right?"

"I got his license plate," I ground out between clenched teeth. Then it hit me what else he'd said. Oh no.

"Wait, what?" Hazel, hands on hips, stared at me. "What person broke in here? When?"

Yikes. Here goes. "Remember when you were staying with Chloe?"

"After she went to the hospital?"

"Yes." I prayed she would forgive me.

"Yes," she said, eyebrows raised, jaw set.

"I came home that night, and someone had broken in and ransacked the house." The words rushed out of me.

"Tell her about CB, Peg." Marcus rubbed the back of his neck.

Hazel knelt beside her dog and hugged him. "What happened?"

"I think he was drugged."

Her eyebrows furrowed.

I held my hand out to her. "He perked up really fast. I was going to take him to the vet to have him checked out, but you saw him the next day when I came to Chloe's. He was fine."

She closed her eyes for several seconds, her nostrils flaring. I sat back on the couch and held my breath, waiting for the explosion. I knew I should have told her long before now.

"You should have told me." Her words mimicked my thoughts.

"You're right. I should have. I'm really sorry." How could I justify what I did. "I shouldn't have kept that from you."

"What else happened," she asked, her gaze stern.

Marcus stepped forward. "They tore up the couch cushions and made a mess in the kitchen. I cleaned it up."

"I managed to stitch up the cushions and flip them." I showed her the underside of the one I sat on.

"Peg,"—Hazel kissed CB—"I'm glad you're okay and so glad this fellow didn't get hurt. But he and Roscoe are my pets. My family. Please don't keep anything like this from me again." The tears on her face broke my heart.

I was hopeful no one would break into my house again, but I kept my mouth shut and simply nodded in agreement.

"What about Roscoe? Hang on." She pushed up from the floor and went to his cage. Turning back to me, she shook her finger. "Birds alive! That's what he's been saying. What he just said. And that's the license plate."

"Yeah, I wondered about that." I hugged a couch pillow. "I'm sorry, Hazel, but I need to lie down. I still don't feel well."

She waved Marcus farther away. "You, move." She helped me put my booted foot on the couch, put a pillow under my head, and smoothed back my hair. "Rest," she whispered. "I'll get rid of him. And then we will talk more." Her last words were delivered with a raised eyebrow and hard stare.

She marched to the front door, holding it wide open. "You have information. Go. Use it. She needs to rest."

"Wait a minute." I pushed up on my elbows. "Why aren't the cops searching for the Bradens, Marcus? This has to have something to do with them."

He pursed his lips, glancing between escape via the front door and me. "I don't know. I was told that by someone higher up."

I cocked an eyebrow. I didn't believe him for a second. He knew, but he wasn't saying.

Marcus rolled his shoulders and headed for the door. He turned around as if he was going to speak, and Hazel slammed the door in his face.

She groaned. "That man."

"Mm-hmm. I'm with you. Thanks for getting rid of him."

"Well, I feel almost the same way about you right now. I'll let you rest, but when you get up, I want the whole story."

I gave her a tired salute and closed my eyes.

MY DREAMS WERE FILLED with cars trying to run over, chase, and pursue me up and down hills and through parking lots. The vehicles were blocky and white. But when I finally woke up, I remembered one black one. And I recognized the make.

"It's an Audi. Hazel,"—I pushed myself up to sit—"it was an Audi. The sedan."

She poked her head around the corner from the kitchen. "What? When did you wake up?"

I ran my fingers through my hair and stretched my neck

side-to-side. "Just now. But I think the car I saw was an Audi. I need to tell Marcus."

"I'm making dinner. Why don't you text him?" She ducked back into the kitchen.

She was cooking? What universe had I woken up to? I rubbed my face and yawned. "What did you say?" A peek into the kitchen showed ground beef browned in a skillet, and a jar of spaghetti sauce sitting on the counter. Water boiled in a pot. A headache popped up between my eyes. "You made dinner?"

She turned from breaking dry noodles into the boiling water. "Yes, of course. I even have some cheese toast."

I pulled out a bar stool and sat. "Sounds good." I tried to catch her eye. "Hazel, why?"

"Why what?"

"Why are you cooking? You haven't cooked since you moved in."

"Sure I have."

"Nope, you haven't. So what's up?"

She pursed her lips. "Tell me what happened today when you went to see Marla."

I recounted my attempted visit.

She lifted the noodle spoon out of the water. "You never saw if it was Marla?"

No, I hadn't. I had assumed it was her. "You're right. I never saw her. The intruder had a pillow over her face."

"Okay, that's an important point. Make sure you tell them that." She turned back to stir the noodles.

"Tell who?"

"Turn the TV on. Check the news."

"Huh?"

She waved the noodle spoon. "Go on. Do it."

I clicked the TV on and turned to the local news channel. And saw my face.

Actually, it was a grainy video clip from the hospital camera outside of the elevator. My heartbeat ramped up. The back of my legs hit the coffee table, and I plopped onto it, staring at the television screen.

"That ... that's me." I pointed. What was going on? Why was my face on TV?

Hazel rushed to my side. "Yes, it is. I've been getting calls all afternoon and saw it on my phone. I didn't know how to tell you." She patted my back. "Take a deep breath."

"I'm trying." Spots appeared in my eyes.

She shoved my head down and waited with me while I calmed down. She tucked my hair behind my ear. "You okay now?"

"Am I a suspect?"

She didn't say anything. I peeked up at her. "Am I?"

She grimaced and clicked her tongue. "Yes? Maybe? Shortie is on his way over. I texted him."

"Oh no." I groaned. I blew out a breath and straightened up, waving Hazel away. "I'm fine." I stood, holding out my arms until the room stopped spinning. "Water would be good."

She handed me a glass. I pointed to the food on the stove. "Is this my last meal?"

"That's not funny." She turned to the stove and stirred the meat and noodles. "But yeah, kind of."

The doorbell rang, and we both hollered, "Come in."

"How are you?" Shortie asked.

"She's making my last meal."

He chuckled. "Ha-ha. They're not going to arrest you."

"You've seen the news? I'm a suspect." My words were panicky.

He sat on the barstool beside me. "No, they want to question you. That's all. I've already talked to Marcus. He wants you to give a statement. I can take you."

I started laughing. I couldn't help it. The Empty Nesters Birding Group had existed for less than a month, and I'd already been questioned about Sylvia's murder. Now I was under suspicion about possibly hurting Marla. It took a few minutes, but I got myself under control with only an occasional burst of mirth slipping out.

Shortie and Hazel didn't say a word.

Hazel plated the spaghetti and added a piece of crunchy cheese toast before she passed around the food. We ate in silence, slurping noodles and chewing bread. When I finished, I wiped my mouth with a napkin and sipped my water.

"I need a few minutes to get ready, and we'll head to the police station." I walked as slowly as I could to my room and shut the door, leaning my head against it.

"How do these things happen to me?" I whispered. Assuming I would be gone for several hours—and making myself not think it might be longer—I brushed my teeth, washed my face, brushed my hair, and changed my clothes. A thought occurred to me, and I hurried to the kitchen.

"Do I need a lawyer?"

Shortie and Hazel's eyes widened.

She stuttered, "I ... I don't know."

He stammered, "Maybe?"

I huffed. "Okay let's get going." I picked up my purse and grabbed my phone. A glance showed several missed texts and calls, mainly from Chloe and Carter. "Hazel, please let the kids know what I'm doing."

She hugged me and whispered, "I'll see you soon." She held the hug longer than usual, and she wiped tears from her cheeks when she stepped away.

I held out my hand to Shortie. "I'll be okay. Let's go."

Marcus and Shortie made my trip to the station as quick and painless as possible. It helped my fingerprints were already on file. I made sure to include I never saw if it was Marla. I wasn't sure if that mattered, but it couldn't hurt. And I included the intruder's threat.

Shortie asked that the news clip be taken down, and Marcus said he'd do his best. I scrolled through social media on the car ride home and knew it would be impossible to stop all the times it had been shared.

I held up my phone. "Oh, this is fun. 'Local mom questioned in attempted murder.'"

"Give me that phone," Shortie growled, grabbing it from me and stuffing it in his door. "It'll die down. Just give it time."

We both knew it would be weeks or months before that happened. Unless we discovered who the real suspect was. I'd told Marcus I thought the black sedan was an Audi, and he said he'd look into it. Maybe he would, but he acted like it was just part of my dream.

We turned onto my street, and I remembered something Shortie had said the week before.

"Didn't you tell us that Estelle had a driver and car that was black?"

He pulled into my driveway. "Yep. Why?"

"You told Marcus that. I was wondering if he ever investigated it. And Charlene said we needed to check out Estelle. Plus, she told us about the vagrant bird her mom spotted."

"Some kind of hummingbird."

Memories and ideas clicked away in my brain. "Yes, a rufous hummingbird. Shortie, the person threatening me and trying to kill Marla has to be Estelle or her driver."

He made a face and turned off his Jeep. He got out and helped me down from my seat, holding onto my hand. "Estelle is in her sixties. I don't think she could do the things that have happened."

I tugged him toward the house. "Ageism."

He chuckled and held his hand out for my keys. "No, not at all. I'm being realistic." He unlocked the door and pushed it open.

"I think we need to try to find Estelle." I set my purse on the island.

"I've looked," Shortie said, holding his hands out. "I never found her, and she didn't attend Sylvia's celebration of life. Let's let the police do their job."

That was something I never thought I'd hear him say. "You are police."

"Well I was." He raked his hand through his hair. "I'm not anymore, Peg. And I have no sway over the Pensacola department or Marcus."

He kissed me goodbye and left. I sat on the couch, flipped the end table lamp on, and tried to read, but I couldn't concentrate. The house was quiet except for the competing snores coming from Hazel's room—I couldn't decipher which were hers and which were CB's. Roscoe shuffled in his cage before he settled. I stared into the dimly lit room, tapping my nails on the end table. Finally, I opened the browser on my phone and typed in Sylvia's name plus rufous hummingbird.

The number of hits that appeared amazed me. I added the words "Estelle Keaton" beside Sylvia's name and tried again. That brought me to one link from a weekly newspaper in California. I clicked it and began to read:

"Last winter, Sylvia Newman and Estelle Keaton discovered the rufous hummingbird in Pensacola, Florida, some 2500 miles from here. The rufous hummingbird is approximately eight centimeters long and often migrates from its breeding grounds in Alaska down to Mexico. The male has bright orange on his back and stomach, plus a red throat. The female has green and orange coloring. Rufous hummingbirds are more aggressive and unafraid to attack other hummingbirds for food.

"According to Mrs. Keaton, finding the vagrant hummingbird was the highlight of her birding career. 'Ms. Newman and I were birding with a few other enthusiasts when we spotted the rufous. I saw him first and pointed him out to my friend. She snapped a picture and submitted the information to the Audubon Society.'"

Estelle found the vagrant bird first? I took a screenshot of the article and texted it to Shortie. This could be the answer. If Estelle was the original spotter, she might have been mad if Sylvia had received all the credit.

But would she be angry enough to kill for that?

Chapter 25

Exhaustion kicked in after I texted Shortie. I plugged my phone in to charge and headed to bed. There was nothing else I could do right now. Except wait to learn more about Sylvia and the vagrant bird, to find out who was in Marla's room, and if Marla had even been there.

As usual, my body was tired when I went to bed, but my brain stayed wide awake. Thoughts swirled and made connections, not always rational, but one did stick and make sense.

Marla was the mayor's wife. If she had been attacked, why wasn't the mayor with her? Why didn't she have some kind of protection? Especially if he planned to run for senator. I couldn't imagine my husband leaving me alone at the hospital after being attacked. That didn't make sense. And, according to Marcus, he had been told Marla and Neil Braden would not be investigated. Less than two weeks before.

I never found out why.

Yet she continued to turn up—at my birding group, my house for coffee, Sylvia's house during her celebration of life.

Estelle Keaton. Marla Braden. Sylvia Newman. These three

women had been a part of each other's lives for years, since high school at least. They entered the Navy together and worked together.

And Estelle and Sylvia birded together. Was Marla with them? When she joined our birding group, she said she'd never birded. But I already knew she wasn't always honest.

Sylvia had an affair and child with Estelle's husband. And she claimed the vagrant hummingbird as her find.

Sylvia was having an affair with Marla's husband at the time of her death.

Wasn't it true that killers kill because of love, money, or jealousy? And Hazel discovered women usually killed someone they knew personally.

Love and jealousy were in play for Sylvia's murder. That much I did know.

THE FOLLOWING day started with someone banging on my front door. I huddled behind the door when I opened it, trying to hide the fact I was still in my PJs.

"Ma'am, we're here to get the tree off of your deck." The man shoved paperwork at me.

I grabbed the front of my robe, blew a strand of hair out of my face, and squinted at the forms.

"Insurance company sent us." His eyes, bracketed by numerous deep squinty lines, were a gorgeous blue.

"Ma'am?" he repeated.

"Yes, that's fine. Back deck. Around back." I slammed the door. "Get hold of yourself, woman." What was up with me and men? I became this nervous Nellie and couldn't put two words together.

Hazel had coffee brewing when I reappeared in clean

clothes, hair and teeth freshly brushed. She handed me a mug and tipped her chin to the back door. The blinds were open, and we watched as the guys cut up and removed the tree from my deck.

"I'm glad that's done," she said. "Maybe my roof will be next."

"I didn't even know they were coming. Have you checked with your insurance?"

We discussed insurance companies while we enjoyed our coffee. Mr. Blue Eyes knocked on the front door and told me they were finished.

"Who does my porch?"

He shrugged. "Not us. Have a good day."

My stomach fluttered at his grin.

"Guess we'll both be checking with our insurance companies," I told Hazel. "Did you see those eyes?"

Hazel giggled. "Yes, I did. But let's focus. You have Shortie."

"And what about Owen for you?"

"Stop now. Tell me what's going on with Marla."

I told her about my thoughts from the night before. "I'm convinced the killer is Estelle or her driver. Could even be Marla, but then who attacked her?"

"Want me to go to the hospital and try to talk to her? We developed a little bit of a friendship, I think. Could she have faked her attack?"

"I'm not sure of anything anymore."

After she left, I cleaned up the house, then called my insurance company who explained it would be a few weeks before someone came about my porch. Too much damage in the surrounding area, they said.

That got me thinking again. I grabbed my keys and purse and got in my car. The hurricane damaged Sylvia's house, and I wanted to see if anyone had taken care of it. Who knew what else I'd discover while I was there? Both Shortie and Marcus wouldn't like the direction of my thoughts, but I wasn't planning to do anything besides look around.

My phone rang while I was driving, and I accepted the call through my wireless earbud. Carter had set it up when I bought the SUV, but I really had no idea how it worked. I said hello and was shocked to hear Marla on the phone.

"Peg? Hi! It's Marla Braden. How are you?"

"I'm fine. Um, how are you? Where are you?" I pulled down Sylvia's driveway and saw the big tree still lying in her backyard.

"I'm good. Feeling better."

Her perky voice set the hairs on the back of my neck to stand at attention. Something was off. "Well, I'm glad. I tried to come see you last night."

"Yes, I thought I heard your voice. There was a little scuffle." Her voice became muffled. "Anyhow, just thought I would say hi."

Hazel should have been to see her by now, but she wasn't mentioning her. After everything that had happened, I was suspicious.

"Did Hazel come to see you?"

Mumbling in the background, then she said, "Yes, she did."

That didn't tell me very much. Something was going on, I knew that. But what it was, I had no idea.

"I just got to Sylvia's. Do you remember what happened here on Monday? Who hurt you?"

"No ... no one hurt me." Her voice trembled, betraying her.

"Are you okay?" I whispered.

"No," she whispered. "I mean, no one hurt me." Her voice grew stronger and more assertive. "Peg, I'm fine, really."

"I'm happy to hear that, Marla. Please tell Hazel I said hello and to call me."

"I'll do that. Goodbye."

She hung up, and I sat in the car, reviewing the few things she said and the background mumbling and noises I had heard. It sounded like a woman's voice, but I couldn't say that for sure. It hadn't been Hazel. And I thought Marla had whispered, "No," in response to my question of if she was okay.

First I would check out Sylvia's house and then call Shortie. He'd told me to leave things to the police, and I assumed that meant Marla.

After I locked my car, I walked around to the backyard. The tree—a tall, skinny pine—was still down. Its top branches stretched to the other side of her lot, and it had narrowly missed the deck. The steep steps were intact. I climbed the stairs and collapsed into one of the Adirondack chairs.

Everything in this case revolved around Sylvia. Nothing had to do with the Empty Nesters Birding Group. Or me. Sylvia was the cause, yet she had died at someone's hand.

Her back door was unlocked. I pushed it, and it slid open. Inside, the house had a stale, empty odor. The mess from when Marla had been accosted had been cleaned up. At least the food was gone. Furniture still stood in odd places. In the corner was a purse. I picked it up.

Inside were Anna's medical alert bracelet and extra EpiPens. My phone rang, and I answered without glancing at the screen.

"Peg? Hi, it's Hazel."

"Hi, I just talked to Marla. How did your visit go?"

"Fine." She paused so long I thought we'd lost our connection.

"Are you there?" I asked. I slung Anna's purse strap on my shoulder and left the house, pulling the sliding door shut.

She inhaled so hard I could hear it. "Yes, I'm here. Well, I was at West Florida Hospital. With Marla. You came to see her last night.”

“Yes, you know I did.”

“That's right, you did. But she's been released.”

Her conversation and tone of voice concerned me. She was acting as evasive as Marla had been.

I paused on the deck. “Do you want me to come to her house?”

“Yes, do that.” Her voice was stern.

“What is going on, Hazel? My phone call with Marla was strange, and so is this one.”

Noises sounded, and then static came through the phone.

“Hazel?” I hobbled down the steep stairway and trotted to my car as fast as my boot allowed. “Hazel!”

The call ended. I buckled my seatbelt and backed out, taking a sharp turn. I punched the call button for Shortie, and relief flowed through my body when his voice came on the line. After explaining the two confusing calls, I told him where I was heading, surprised at myself for remembering Marla's address. He assured me he'd be there as soon as possible but was in Pace, which would take a bit.

“Call the police if you're really worried,” he said.

“I will.” He let me go, and I sped down I-10 and turned right onto Davis Highway, grumbling at the crazy intersection and drivers. Just past the hospital was a small, older neighborhood where the Bradens lived. Marla had written her address the day she came for coffee. That day felt like years ago. I spotted Hazel's yellow car and pulled into the driveway.

I exited my SUV and glanced up and down the street. No sound, no neighbors outside. My stomach clenched, and my mouth was dry as beach sand. I forced myself to knock on the door.

No answer. I tapped again, and the door swung in. “Hello?”

Music played in my head. The frightening kind used in movies just before the actress did something stupid. I took one step into the foyer, stopping to listen.

Nothing. Complete silence. Then, a shuffle, a mumble, a grunt.

The grunt was familiar. I shoved the door farther and rushed inside. Hazel sat in the corner of the living room, a gag stuffed in her throat, a torn sheet holding her in a chair. Marla was lying on the couch, also gagged and tied down. Both women's eyes were huge, and they were both struggling to talk.

Hazel's gag was a bright yellow non-skid sock, the kind hospitals use. "Yuck. Let's take that out. Who did this to you?"

She swung her head back and screamed, with little sound coming out from around the sock. She attempted to wave her arms. All I saw before my world went black was her finger pointing behind me.

My HEAD HURTS. That was my first thought when I managed to open my eyes. My arms wouldn't move when I tried to reach up and rub it. Something was stuck in my mouth. I used my tongue to push it out, but it wouldn't budge. I squeezed my eyes shut and reopened them, and the room came into focus.

Hazel sat in the corner, still tied down, tears streaming down her face. Marla lay still, a gag in her mouth. From what I could see, I was in a different corner of the room, and out of the edge of my eye, a yellow sock—probably the mate to Hazel's—was in my mouth. My arms and legs were tied up with a torn sheet.

"Awake, I see." A slender man walked in front of me and leaned over. "You are a troublemaker. Always in the way.

Always snooping and sticking your nose into things." He poked his finger in my face.

I tried to ask who he was, but it sounded like Charlie Brown's teacher in the Peanuts comic, "Wah, wah, wah."

"Nope. I'll tell you what you need to know." He straightened up and approached Marla. He ran his fingers down her cheek. "This is my wife. Marla Braden." He turned and patted his puffed-out chest. "I am her husband, Neil Braden."

If it could, my mouth would have dropped open. I frowned and struggled against the torn sheets he'd used to bind me to the chair.

He winked. "You have questions?"

Chapter 26

Yes, I had questions! I tried to say that, but only a nod conveyed my words. This man, this skinny, self-righteous man, was Neil Braden? Our mayor and potential senator?

Those weren't the only questions running through my mind, but they were at the top of my list.

Neil tipped his head and tapped his chin. His movements made me wonder if he was on something, some kind of drug. I risked a peek at Hazel, whose expression was so sad. She knew we were in trouble. A glance at Marla made me realize she hadn't moved or woken up since I'd been knocked out.

I gestured with my chin toward her.

He leered—a nasty Joker-like expression—and approached her again.

"You're wondering about my wife?"

"Uh-huh."

He scooched up on the couch and stretched out beside her. She didn't move. "She's fine don't worry. I just gave her a little something to calm her." He kissed her cheek, then snapped his fingers and hopped off the bed.

This guy was all over the place. His jerky, uncoordinated movements scared me, and I didn't know how to read him or anticipate what he would do. He pulled a chair closer to me, turned it around, and straddled it. He leaned closer, his overpowering aftershave, stale breath, and anxious sweat making me want to vomit. I jerked my head away when he tried to touch me.

He cocked an eyebrow. "Not playing, huh? Okay here's the deal. You got in the middle of something. Sylvia was the problem. I know you read those emails and letters. Marla told me." He blew a kiss in his wife's direction.

Hazel whimpered, and I turned to her. I tried to signal peace and calm with my eyes. I knew Shortie was on the way, but she didn't. *Hurry, Shortie, please.* I tuned back into Neil's tirade.

"So, back in the day, Marla, Estelle Keaton, and Sylvia were friends. Really good friends. They graduated together, went into the Navy together, and Sylvia flew up in rank. She out-worked and out-paced her 'friends.'" He made air quotes. "She was something else." His eyes gleamed.

"She was beautiful, and she knew it. Used it to her advantage. Had an affair with Roger while he was married to Estelle. This happened before he became such a legend. Estelle hated her." He stood and shoved the chair away, pacing the room.

"Keaton bought her that huge house. Estelle became furious. Then, the women went birding together. Marla too. They all pretended to be friends, but I knew the truth. See, back then, dear Estelle confided in me. Told me things. We spent time together." His expression was slimy. I knew what he was saying.

"On one birding trip, Estelle found a new bird in the area. A vagrant bird, I think they call them. Sylvia took a picture and sent the information to the Audubon Society. Guess what? She didn't use Estelle's name. At all. Boy, was that woman mad."

Hazel whimpered again, and Neil jerked around, shaking his finger in her face. "You. Hush. No one's going to rescue you. So, for now, it's just me, you, and you. Oh, and Marla. That's right, let's get back to my story." He perched on the edge of the couch, one knee crossed over the other, and fished in his pocket. "It's a good story, right?"

My eyes were fixed on what he'd pulled out. It could be a pen, but it was different.

He waved it at me. "You like? It's a tactical pen made especially for me." He showed off its features, running his finger over the sharp, pointy end. "This will come in very handy."

Out of the corner of my eye, I saw Marla's lashes fluttering. I kept my gaze on Neil's face.

"So blah, blah, blah, birding, Charlene, blah, blah, Estelle. Yes, she was angry. She wanted to get even. But she took her time. She planned. And waited. She knew Sylvia had a peanut allergy and asked me to switch that birdseed. No problem, I told her." He waved the pen as he talked. "Only that other girl died. That Annie girl."

"Anna," I screamed. Only nothing but mumbles came out.

"You'll be glad to know I put an obit in the paper for her. Anna Thompson." He saw my expression. "Yes, I know her real name. No one ever asked about her body or anything. I have people in the police department. People who tell me … things. So, I took the matter into my hands and called the obituary line for the *Pensacola News Journal,* and that was that." He set his pen beside him and brushed his hands together.

Things were coming together now. Neil was behind all of this and had stooges on the police force who fed him information—and kept him and his wife from being investigated. Sorrow over doubting Marcus filled me.

But I remembered something. I had Anna's purse, and in it were EpiPens—three of them. And I knew if you use an EpiPen and don't need it, the medicine can make you sick. Sometimes really sick. What would all three of them do to Neil if I could get to them and him?

I wiggled my hand. He had tied me just above my wrist to the arm of a wooden chair. I could move my fingers and my wrist. I felt for the purse and unzipped it. Now to reach the EpiPens, uncap them, get Neil close enough, and stick him with all three.

No problem.

I caught Hazel's eye and tried to signal she needed to distract Neil. Too bad I didn't know Morse code. She cocked her head, watching me. I could tell when she saw the purse and my hand in it. Her gaze flew to my face, she inhaled, and then stomped her feet and rocked her chair, making as much noise as possible.

Neil jumped up and got in her face. "Stop it," he whispered in a harsh tone. He poked the pen at her before putting his hands on her wrists and pushing her chair down.

Her face paled, and my stomach clenched.

"Don't hurt her," I tried to scream around my gag. I rocked my chair, and my hand slid farther into the purse. I managed to grab two of the EpiPens and used my thumb to pop the caps off. I continued to rock my chair and stomp my feet, hoping help would arrive. How long had it been since I called Shortie?

Marla sat straight up, her gag popped out, and she screamed. Neil rushed over to me. When he was close enough, I shoved two EpiPens in his thigh. The door to the house flew open, and Shortie ran in. He grabbed Neil around the neck, put him in a chokehold, and knocked the tactical pen away. Neil grabbed his chest and slumped in Shortie's arms.

~

THE POLICE CAME and took Shortie and me for questioning. Because of Hazel's age, she had to go by ambulance to be seen by a doctor. Marla had to return to the hospital until they determined she was safe, and whatever drug Neil had given her had worn off.

Neil was another story. The EpiPens sent him into shock. His heart was fine, but he thought he was having a heart attack. If I'd managed to grab the third EpiPen, it might not have turned out that way.

I was thankful I'd only used two. Even with all the horrible things he had done, I didn't want to be a killer.

An officer took me to a room, and after a minute, Marcus entered. I sat, crossed my arms, and waited. Body language no longer mattered. Neil had confessed—at least to Anna's murder.

Marcus studied me. He opened his mouth several times, but no words came out.

I took pity on him. "Do you want to know what Neil told me?"

He nodded and grabbed a pad of paper and a pen. "Go ahead."

"He confessed to switching the birdseed at Sylvia's. He also had an affair with Sylvia at some point. And Estelle, too, I think. He told me he has help within the police department."

Marcus's eyebrows rose.

"Yep. He put an obituary in the paper for Anna, and he made sure he and Marla wouldn't be any part of an investigation."

"Okay. Excuse me a moment." He left the room, and when he returned, his face was several shades paler. He picked up his notepad. "Where were we? Tell me more about Neil."

I had been bound and determined to pin it all on Estelle. Neil never was a real suspect. She was a part of it, though. I told Marcus.

"So, Estelle asked Neil to put that seed in there? The one with the peanuts?" he asked.

"Yes, but where is she? I've never seen her or met her."

He leaned forward, elbows propped on the table between us. "As far as we can tell, she skipped town. I assume she's in Guatemala with Keaton."

"Hmm. Has Neil confessed to anything else? Killing Sylvia?"

"I can't tell you that." He leaned back.

"Yeah. Neil also mentioned the birding problem. The vagrant bird."

"You lost me there."

I explained about the vagrant bird spotting—the rufous hummingbird—and what that meant in the birding community. I told him how Sylvia had claimed the rights to it, even though Estelle had actually seen the bird before her.

"If you search online for their names and the hummingbird, you'll find an old newspaper article that states Estelle saw it first."

"That would make her kill Sylvia?" Marcus's voice was incredulous. "I'll never understand these bird wackos."

"Hey!" I took offense at that. I was a birder now. Some of my best friends were bird watchers. "We're not all crazy. Just look at me and Hazel and Shortie."

He cocked an eyebrow and said nothing.

"Pfft." I waved my hand at him.

He tapped his pen on the notebook. "Anything else you can tell me?"

"Do you have any information on Marla?" I asked.

"Last I heard from the hospital, Marla is recovering nicely. She had a concussion from when she got hurt at Sylvia's."

"I guess Neil had her stop there."

"That's what I think." He pinched his lips together.

"Ha! You told me something!" I pumped my fist in the air.

He slapped his notepad on the table. "I have officially lost control of this interview." He smiled. "I want to say something off the record."

I glanced around the tiny room. "Don't you need to stop the camera or whatever?"

He chuckled. "No, I don't have one on. I believe you, Peg. You're a good person." He paused and cleared his throat. "I'm sorry I came on so strong, especially about Shortie. He's a good guy. He's lucky to have you."

Tears prickled. "Thank you." Maybe I should apologize for suspecting him of impeding the investigation, but I didn't.

He patted my hand and stood. "Come on. Let's get you out of here."

"Yes, I want to check on Hazel."

"I forgot to tell you, but she is fine. No problems. I think one of our guys brought her here, and after she gives her statement, y'all can go home."

"Thank God. I was so worried about her."

We left the room, and he showed me to the waiting area. Shortie sat, knee jumping up and down, fingers tapping on the table beside him. He saw me and hopped up.

"I'm so glad you're okay." He brushed my hair back. "You are, right? I couldn't believe when I got to the house, and Braden had you." He wrapped me in a warm hug.

"Yes, I'm fine," I whispered in his ear.

He led me to a chair, and we sat beside each other, holding hands. I told him what had happened and what I'd told Marcus.

"So Braden switched the birdseed? Who killed Sylvia and made those calls to you? Who hurt Marla?"

"And, who broke into my house and taught Roscoe to say, 'Birds Alive!'?"

Someone cleared their throat, and we turned. Hazel waved. "I think I can answer those questions."

Chapter 27

We were all starving. Shortie made what he called a command decision and drove through the drive-through of the sandwich shop. He even got three of their kitchen sink cookies, saying we deserved it after what we went through.

"Cookies are self-care, right?" I said.

At my house, Hazel let an anxious CB out to do his thing, and I tossed Roscoe some seed. He stayed in his corner, and I stayed in mine. I blew him a kiss when I finished. CB came in, and Hazel set a bowl of chow down for him.

Shortie laid our food out on the dining table. Once we'd all washed our hands, we sat to eat. Hazel grabbed my hand and one of Shortie's before we started.

She bowed her head. "Dear Lord, thank You, thank You. You kept us safe today. You provided what we needed. Thank You." She squeezed our hands, then picked up a napkin and dabbed at her eyes. "What a day."

"Crazy day." I unwrapped my sandwich and took a bite. "Yum."

Shortie slid a bag of chips my way.

"Thank you. I plan to eat this whole sandwich, the chips, and my cookie. Then, you can tell us everything." I mumbled around my food and pointed to Hazel.

The house was quiet as everyone ate. Shortie finished first, threw his trash away, grabbed his cookie, and took CB back outside. Hazel and I cleaned up our trash when we were done.

I sipped my water. "I'm saving my cookie. I feel better now, but I want to enjoy it later. I still have such a headache." I rubbed my temples.

She leaned against the kitchen counter. "Me too. I never imagined this day would turn out like this. Have you checked your phone yet? I know the kids wanted to talk to you. Lauree too."

"Oh no, my poor kids." My phone showed multiple missed calls and texts from Chloe and Carter. I shot a quick message to assure them I was home and safe and would call soon. I copied and pasted it to send to Lauree. All three answered immediately, seeming to believe my reassuring text.

Shortie and CB came inside, and we settled in the living room—Shortie and I on the couch and Hazel in the lounge chair. CB stretched out on the carpet at Hazel's feet and sighed.

"He's glad you're home."

She rubbed his tummy with her foot. "Me too." She nestled back into the chair and closed her eyes.

"No way." I leaned over and tapped her arm. "You don't get to go to sleep yet. We have questions, and you said you'd answer them." I crossed my arms.

Shortie held up his hand and counted on his fingers. "Who killed Sylvia, who called Peg, who hurt Marla, who broke into the house."

I jumped in before he could finish, "Who says, 'Birds alive!' and drove the black car?"

Hazel made a shushing motion. "Neil answered most of

that before you got there, Peg. He was crazy. When I first got to Marla's house, the lights were dim, and she was asleep. I set my purse on a chair and waited. She woke up and saw me, but she looked so frightened. She kept mouthing words to me. I couldn't understand her though."

"Was it Neil? Was he there?" I asked.

"Yes. He had hidden down the hall in the bathroom. Marla wouldn't, or couldn't, say much—I guess she was scared of him."

"I'm sure she was," I said. "He put her in the hospital in the first place."

Yes, he was quite happy about what he'd done."

"What a creep."

"And so weird. He talked so strangely. Like he was on something."

"That's what I thought. His mannerisms were very odd." I glanced at Shortie. "Did you hear him say anything when you came in?"

"No, I saw him standing over you with that knife thingy, and I grabbed him. I probably would've killed him if I hadn't controlled myself." He wrung his hands.

I patted his leg and pulled his hands apart, holding onto one. "I don't think so. That's not who you are."

His shoulders relaxed, and he pulled me close. "Thank you." He kissed my temple.

Hazel cleared her throat. "Do you want to hear more?"

"Yes." I gestured to her to continue.

"Okay, so Neil came out of the bathroom, acting and talking strangely. He tied me up and gagged me. Then he did the same to Marla. I was so afraid for her. He told me he'd called her to stop at Sylvia's after she left here the night of the celebration of life."

"That makes sense. When she left the house here, we thought she was going straight to the funeral home."

"Neil said when she arrived at Sylvia's, he was dressed up as an intruder and clubbed her over the head."

How could he do that to his wife? I remembered what Hazel had said, that he was known to have had multiple affairs. My heart broke for Marla.

Hazel continued. "He ran off before we arrived for the refreshments. He confessed to killing Sylvia, but he tried to blame it on Estelle."

"He told us about switching the birdseed that killed Anna, remember?"

"Yes, but he blamed Estelle for everything he said he did. He said they'd had an affair."

"That was years before." I shifted on the couch and propped my boot on the coffee table.

"Are you hurting?" Shortie asked.

"Ibuprofen would help." I told him where it was, and he offered some to Hazel.

She waved it away. "I need some sleep. That will do the trick."

I swallowed the pills. "We know Neil killed Sylvia. Did he mention the threatening phone calls I got?"

"He said Estelle made them."

Shortie frowned and pulled his phone from his pocket. "I'm going to text Marcus and have him check into that. They should be able to pull Braden's phone records."

Hazel waited until he put his phone down. "Neil did say he was driving Estelle's car, but he never mentioned breaking into the house. I never heard him say birds alive or anything like that."

Roscoe piped up and offered his newest words, "Birds alive!"

"We got it, buddy." I grinned. "At least it's not more of his potty mouth."

We all laughed. Shortie rubbed his hand over the back of his neck and stood.

"I'm heading home." He yawned and stretched.

I walked him out, and he waited until I got into the house and shut the door. I locked it and blinked the front porch light so he'd know we were safe inside. I finished my cookie and headed to bed. Tomorrow would be here soon enough.

FIRST THING THE NEXT MORNING, I called Chloe and Carter and filled them in. They had both seen my picture on the TV and were worried. I explained the only loose end was Estelle.

And that bothered me. But I didn't tell them that.

Lauree came over after lunch. I told her what I'd told the kids and also my concerns about Estelle.

Hazel heard me and added her two cents. "She's as unstable as Neil Braden from what he said."

"I don't understand how he could do those things." Lauree exclaimed, her voice shaking. "And you two could have been killed!"

"Calm down. We're okay." I patted her leg.

"What are you going to do about Estelle?" she asked.

Good question. I had no idea.

Hazel switched the television on. "I want to forget about all of it. It's over." She clicked over to the news channel.

A news ticker at the bottom of the screen read, "Breaking News," and Estelle's picture appeared. The off-camera reporter said, "Estelle Keaton, the wife of Pensacola's infamous Roger Keaton, is sought in connection with several recent murders. Last night, police arrested Pensacola Mayor Neil Braden as an accomplice of Mrs. Keaton's. The Pensacola Police Department issued a statement saying they needed to talk to Mrs. Keaton as soon as possible. If anyone has any information, please call Crime Stoppers." She rattled off the phone number.

A video of Estelle from a party came on the screen. I squinted and leaned forward. "Turn up the TV, Hazel."

The video ran. It was from when Neil Braden declared his bid to run for senator. Red, white, and blue balloons, plus a banner, hung all around the room. Estelle and Neil were talking to Roger Keaton, Marla hovering at Braden's elbow. I couldn't hear Estelle speaking, but I watched her mouth and saw her say, "Birds alive."

I sucked in a breath. "Did y'all see what I just saw?"

"Looked like she said, 'Birds alive,'" Lauree said.

"Yep. I think she did," Hazel agreed.

I texted Shortie and Marcus, telling them what channel we were watching and what we'd seen.

"I guess that wraps up all the mystery," Lauree said.

I chuckled. "I don't think so." I pointed to the TV where the next reporter was talking about a missing quetzal. A map of Central and South America appeared that included a picture of the missing bird.

"What's a quetzal?" Hazel asked.

"Shush, listen."

"Only about 50,000 of these beautiful birds still exist. Usually found in the highlands of Guatemala, they're also found in Mexico and Central America." The reporter shifted and pointed to the map. "They live in tropical forests, or what's called 'cloud forests,' and they hop between the trees. The International Union for the Conservation of Nature considers the quetzal as a near threatened species because of their decreased population."

The female news anchor in the studio added, "That's why they're so concerned about the missing quetzal."

"Definitely." The reporter nodded. "Plus, quetzals do not do well in captivity. Right now, only two zoos have the bird in their collection."

The news anchor wore a disgusted expression. "We'll keep you updated on the missing quetzal." She turned the rest of the news over to the weatherman, and Hazel switched off the TV.

"What a beautiful bird," Lauree said. "Such a long, colorful tail."

"It is gorgeous." I paused. "But, Guatemala?" I stared at Lauree and Hazel. "That's where Keaton is supposed to be."

"And maybe Estelle. I wonder if that's why she's there? Maybe she's up to another birding mishap," Hazel said.

"Where is she?" I asked.

Hazel lifted her hands. "And, more important, where's the quetzal?"

THE END

Acknowledgments

I've read that books are a team effort—and it's true. My grateful thanks to all my writing friends and co-conspirators in this world of words, especially to my first mentor, Larry Leech, for his encouragement and guidance, and to the Scribes201 critique group for their patience with me. Y'all rock.

Without my family, I wouldn't be the person I am. So, thank you, Eddie—my love, my heart, my BFF. And my kiddos who have cheered me on when I sent screenshots of word counts and then when I typed, 'The End.' And my grands, who don't really understand what it means that I wrote a book. But one day, they will.

My dad—how I wish you could see this book. You believed in me and always had my back. My mom—what a blessing to be a librarian's daughter. You've helped me brainstorm so many times, and your love for your family is awe-inspiring. My brother and sister—your love, prayers, and friendship mean more than you know. Sorry about hitting you with the cap gun.

To my other friends and family who listen to me ramble about all things writing and even ask me how it's going— Thank you!

About the Author

Jen Dodrill is married and is the mother of five adult children and grandmother of three, two girls and a boy. She homeschooled for thirteen years, taught Oral Communication for her local community college, and is a 'retired' Navy wife. After her youngest graduated high school, Jen started writing her first book. Her inspiration comes in many forms, and she loves incorporating humor and personal experiences into her stories.

Jen is an avid fiction reader with an eclectic collection of novels, many of which sit in an old embalming fluids box belonging to her great-grandfather, Captain Alfred, MD.

When she's not writing, you'll find her spending time with her family or curled up on the couch with her favorite black cat, reading and drinking a mug of dark roast coffee.

To learn more, visit her website —https://jendodrillwrites.com

You May Also Like ...

Show Me Betrayal by Ellen E. Withers

Show Me Mysteries—Book One

Two deaths occur decades apart. Is it possible these deaths are related? What motivates a killer, who got away with murder sixty years ago, to kill again? Was it uncontrollable rage or the hope of silencing someone who fit all the puzzle pieces together and deduced who committed the crime?

Set in the picturesque town of Mexico, Missouri, *Show Me Betrayal* takes flight in words and emotions of rich characters woven together into a story you won't want to put down.

Get your copy here:

https://scrivenings.link/showmebetrayal

The Case of Misaken Identity by Deborah Sprinkle

A Mac & Sam Mystery—Book Two

Private Investigator Mackenzie Love manages to get into trouble on a simple shopping trip where she finds herself at the business end of a gun. It's clear her attacker mistakes her for someone else, but who? And why is her look-alike in so much trouble?

Mac enlists the help of her partners, Samantha Majors and Miss P, and Detective Jake Sanders to find her doppelgänger and solve the case of mistaken identity.

In the meantime, Mr. Fischer of Fischer Industries comes to the private detectives for help with a problem of his own. As Mac and Sam work on his case, they begin to wonder if the two cases are related.

Can Mac and Sam unravel the clues and get justice for both Mac's look-alike and Mr. Fischer?

Get your copy here:

https://scrivenings.link/mistakenidentity

❧

Manicures and Murder by Keri Lynn

A Texas-Sized Mystery—Book Three

When Lacey Baker's best friend is murdered only weeks before Christmas, the salon owner realizes that not all is what it seems in her small town. After an attempt is made on her own life, Lacey finds herself not only thrust back into the world of rodeo she thought she'd left behind, but also into the arms of her ex-fiancé, Cody. With time running out, one mistake is all it will take for everything to come undone.

Get your copy here:

https://scrivenings.link/manicuresandmurder

Stay up-to-date on your favorite books and authors with our free e-newsletters.

ScriveningsPress.com

www.ingramcontent.com/pod-product-compliance
Lightning Source LLC
Chambersburg PA
CBHW070632100726
47907CB00007B/1951